A FAMILY AFFAIR

When Harriet Maxwell, a divorced headteacher, spends the summer with her family in Spain, she falls in love with Carlos Mendoza: a widower with four children. But Harriet faces a dilemma: Zoe, her teenaged daughter, also falls for Carlos; the forthcoming marriage announcement cannot be made. Her predicament gets complicated when a misunderstanding prompts Carlos to leave. As Harriet copes with various family problems, and bonds with his children, she fears she will never see Carlos again.

MEL VINCENT

A FAMILY AFFAIR

Complete and Unabridged

LINFORD
Leicester

First published in Great Britain in 1986 by
Robert Hale Limited
London

First Linford Edition
published 2006
by arrangement with
Robert Hale Limited
London

British Library CIP Data

Vincent, Mel
A family affair.—Large print ed.—
Linford romance library
1. Love stories
2. Large type books
I. Title
823.9'14 [F]

ISBN 1–84617–414–7

Published by
F. A. Thorpe (Publishing)
Anstey, Leicestershire

Set by Words & Graphics Ltd.
Anstey, Leicestershire
Printed and bound in Great Britain by
T. J. International Ltd., Padstow, Cornwall

This book is printed on acid-free paper

1

With a sigh of relief Harriet buckled her seat belt, closed her eyes and braced herself for the take-off. 'At last,' she breathed, scarcely able to believe, after all the hitches and last-minute arrangements, she was on her way. She could relax and enjoy herself for the next six weeks and try to forget the traumas of the last year. What bliss to be able to shed her responsibilities . . .

At least most of her responsibilities. She opened her eyes reluctantly and let them rest on the occupant of the seat next to hers. Zoe, her seventeen-year-old daughter was looking out of the window, a sullen expression on her pretty face. The long, silky, blonde hair had fallen forward but Harriet could see the drooping mouth and sense the tension in her daughter's slight figure.

She touched Zoe's hand. 'Your seat

belt, dear.' Impatiently, the young girl buckled her belt. Another restriction, her manner plainly conveyed, then she turned her face to the window again to watch the disappearing lights on the ground as the aeroplane rose into the sky.

Harriet resettled herself in her seat, controlling the tide of irritation that Zoe's moods often triggered in her. 'She's had a bad time lately — haven't we all! But Zoe has reacted particularly badly to the divorce.' Harriet's thoughts wandered on as the roar of the aircraft's engines changed to a quiet hum. 'She adores her father. Funny how he has that effect on everybody. Even me, for the first few years of our marriage, until I began to see his other side. I hope neither she nor Ben find out that side of their father.'

She could still feel the surge of relief when Roger had finally left last year. She wondered, not for the first time, if she'd been wrong in keeping up the pretence, trying to protect the children from disillusion. A small sigh escaped her. After all that time she could hardly tell them the truth now. They wouldn't believe her, especially since Roger typically got *his* explanation to them first, blaming her for putting her career first, before himself and the children. How were they to know it was the money from her teaching jobs that kept the family solvent in the early years and then paid for those small extras that so soon became essentials in their lives?

She paid for their annual holidays by the sea, a car for Roger, clothes for them all, but most important — a good education for both children. Ben had gone through University with flying colours and Zoe had been accepted and would start after the summer holiday. It was quite an achievement and Harriet was proud of them both, but without her career and the money it brought, University would have been a tremendous financial burden.

Roger had contributed spasmodically

towards household expenses, his various business ventures usually ending in failure because of his lack of foresight and business sense. Harriet had even paid off a large debt to keep him out of the law courts.

There had been other women, too. No-one guessed, least of all Harriet, and she would have remained in ignorance had not Roger amused himself after they had been married several years by deliberately leaving evidence of his affairs for her to find. When confronted he would deny everything, explain plausibly in his charming way, but leaving no doubt in Harriet's mind that he was lying.

'Would you like a drink, madam?' A voice interrupted Harriet's dreary thoughts and she looked up at the stewardess with relief.

'A gin and tonic, please,' she answered forcing a bright smile and turning to her daughter. 'What would you like to drink, Zoe?' Getting no response, she said quickly to the waiting stewardess: 'She'll have bitter lemon, please.'

When their drinks had been brought Harriet sat upright in her seat, addressing her daughter crisply: 'That was a lovely exhibition of bad manners. I hope you're feeling better now.'

Zoe slowly turned her face from the window and poured her drink into the clear plastic beaker. 'I'm sorry.' There was a break in her voice and, in spite of her anger, Harriet felt a rush of sympathy for her confused, unhappy daughter. She tried a more reasonable tone, pulling at a curly tendril of her short dark hair, a habit from childhood still practised when she was tense or agitated. 'You'll pull the curl out of your hair,' her mother used to rebuke her, but here she was, forty years later, still blessed with curls at a period when all the latest styles were for straight hair!

'Look, Zoe, I know you'd been looking forward to going to the Greek

Islands with those new friends of yours. If you'd had some definite plans of where you were staying I might have agreed, but it was all so vague. I know you're nearly eighteen and other young people do it. We've been through that. I'm not allowing it! I don't even know these new friends of yours. You haven't brought them home although you know they're welcome.'

Zoe muttered something under her breath which her mother couldn't hear, but she guessed it would be something about being old-fashioned.

Harriet went on undeterred: 'You wouldn't listen to any of my suggestions for a holiday. You showed no interest until less than a week ago when you suddenly announced you'd like to go to Emily's villa in Spain. I've been 'phoning airlines every day and it was pure luck I managed to get these cancelled seats. We spent all day yesterday shopping for clothes for you and I'm absolutely shattered. Now all you can do is sulk and moan and be as rude as you can. I wish I'd not bothered.'

All this was conducted in undertones as Harriet was aware of the proximity of other passengers, but the anger and frustration which crept into her voice at last conveyed its message to Zoe, who looked at her mother in surprise. Harriet had always been a strict mother as her ban on the Greek holiday confirmed, but neither Zoe, nor her brother Ben had ever seen their mother lose her temper. She was always cool in a crisis, calm but firm in any minor family arguments and even in the last traumatic year had always appeared to be in control of herself and her feelings.

'Sorry, Mum,' repeated Zoe, this time really sounding as if she meant it. For the first time she seemed to notice the shadows beneath her mother's sapphire blue eyes and the pallor of exhaustion of her lovely face. Zoe went on: 'It's just that I hate going around on my own on holiday. Ben's usually there to go to discos with and Dad . . . We've always been a family. It seems so strange — just the two of us.'

Harriet smiled sympathetically at her daughter. 'I know how you feel, love, but we'll just have to make the best of it. There are sure to be other young people there, Segena's becoming quite a popular resort according to Emily.'

'But what about you, Mum?' asked Zoe. 'What will you do with yourself? You won't know anyone either.'

'That will be just perfect for me. I want to be where I don't know anyone, where I can sit and read — novels, thrillers, pure escapist stuff, in fact, anything that has nothing to do with education,' she said with a mischievous smile at her daughter. 'I shall sleep in the sun every day, do as little housework as possible and . . . wallow in idleness.' Her voice sounded blissful at the prospect and Zoe grinned back.

Harriet had the disturbing thought that at this moment she and Zoe seemed closer than they'd been for over a year and it was all due to the fact that she, Harriet, had inadvertently let her desperation and unhappiness show. She knew in a sudden flash of insight that she had been wrong to try to shoulder the burden of the last year alone. The children were now grown up and she should have confided in them more; not necessarily to tell them the whole truth of her marriage, or travesty of a marriage, it was too late for that, but to show them that things were not easy for her, that she had her problems too and that she was not always as calm and strong as she tried to appear.

'Anyway,' she now consoled her daughter, 'we shan't be on our own for long. Ben's hoping to come later this week. He and Gabrielle are leaving London on Thursday and driving through France and Spain. They'll be with us by the week-end.'

Zoe was unenthusiastic. 'It won't be the same. I always feel Gabrielle resents me when I go around with them.'

'I suppose that's natural with an engaged couple, but I'm sure you're wrong about Gabrielle's attitude to you, she's always very pleasant.'

'Pleasant, yes, but not exactly friendly.'

'That's only her way. I shouldn't take any notice. Try to like her, Zoe. Ben's so fond of her and I know you wouldn't like to hurt him.'

'He's potty about her, that's what make me so sick. She treats him like dirt sometimes and he just takes it. I don't know what's got into him, he's usually so positive and independent.'

Harriet made no response to this because secretly she felt it was true. She wasn't altogether happy about her son's choice of future wife — a successful model in London. Her cool manner both towards Ben's mother and sister had not endeared her to either of them, but Harriet was too loyal to her son to allow her own lack of enthusiasm to show.

Zoe continued: 'I'm surprised she's coming. She hates the sun and the sea. She told me once the sun makes her skin and hair dry, and I can't imagine her going in the sea.'

Harriet allowed herself a small smile at the thought of the immaculate and elegant Gabrielle cavorting in the sea with a beach-ball as Ben and Zoe did.

She thought of Ben, so like herself, with dark brown curly hair and deep blue eyes. He, too, had her keen sense of humour, often hidden by their quiet, thoughtful manner. They often took people by surprise with their sudden flashes of wit and whimsy. Harriet found this trait in herself had helped her get through the worst moments of her life. She usually managed to find something of the ridiculous in the darkest situation and often that amusement was directed at herself. That this was a defence mechanism used to hide her true feelings never occurred to her and would have shocked her deeply.

Zoe, favouring her father, was emotional, volatile and restless. She had his charm of manner and could be completely captivating, or, thought

Harriet wryly, absolutely impossible. Harriet loved her daughter deeply but often worried about Zoe's adoration of her father. She knew that if Zoe ever witnessed her father's less endearing traits, which he'd always been very careful to hide from his children, she would be devastated. Zoe hadn't the strength her mother had developed over the difficult years of her marriage.

'I mustn't keep going over all this. I'm on holiday and *nobody* is going to spoil it for me!' With that determined thought in her mnd Harriet consciously relaxed her taut body and finished her gin and tonic.

Zoe had suddenly come to life and was humming a gay little tune to herself. For a moment Harriet was taken by surprise as she often was by Zoe and her father's sudden changes of mood, until she followed her daughter's glance and noticed that the occupant of the adjoining seat was an extremely attractive Spanish boy of Zoe's own age.

'Would you like to sit by the window for a while, Mum?' Zoe asked with an entrancing smile at the obviously fascinated young man.

Harriet willingly changed seats. Content that Zoe had found a congenial travelling companion for the rest of the journey, she closed her eyes and, at last, drifted off to sleep.

* * *

As always the sight of the villa lightened Harriet's weary spirits. Set in an idyllic landscaped complex of a dozen or so villas, each of unique design and with its own swimming-pool, it seemed like paradise, compared to the dreary, rain-washed streets of London so recently abandoned.

The villa belonged to Emily Preston, former Headmistress of Larkhill Primary School in the East End of London, where Harriet had been her Deputy for several years. A close friendship had grown between the two women in spite of an age difference of nearly twenty years.

Emily was Harriet's guide and mentor in her career and was the only person who knew the true state of the marriage between the younger woman and Roger Maxwell. Her sympathy and integrity made her the ideal confidante to whom Harriet was able to unburden herself when the situation at home became unbearable. Emily knew Harriet would never allow her personal problems to interfere with her job and respected both her courage and her dedication to teaching the young children from an area notorious for its social problems.

Emily herself had no easy life. She supported an elderly invalid mother who had been widowed after only five years of marriage, and a younger sister whose health was also poor. In spite of her sacrifices, having broken off a youthful engagement because of her responsibilities towards her family, she had a lively, if rather ironic sense of humour and a down-to-earth practical manner which refused to foster regrets for what might have been.

When Emily's mother suddenly died two years ago, she was amazed to learn that a considerable amount of money had been secreted away by that lady, unknown to either of her daughters.

Emily sought Harriet's advice: 'What on earth shall I do with all that money? I could have done with it before, when I was trying to stretch my salary to support the three of us. What was she thinking about?' Emily shrugged her shoulders helplessly, for once finding herself in a situation which left her unable to make up her mind.

'Perhaps she was doing it for your sake, so you could both live in comfort, not to say luxury, now she's gone,' replied Harriet diplomatically.

'You know better than that,' replied Emily wryly. Harriet smiled — she'd known Emily's mother, a lady not renowned for her charitable thoughts even towards her own daughters.

'Why don't you spend it — enjoy yourselves. You and Beatrice could travel.'

'It's a bit late for us to go gadding round the world.'

'Nonsense. You deserve to have some fun, Emily. Life hasn't exactly been a round of pleasure for you so far. Go on, do it before it *is* too late. Or, why don't you buy a villa in Spain or Portugal?'

The idea must have taken shape in Emily's mind, for a few weeks later she astounded Harriet by announcing she had decided to retire and was in the process of buying a villa on the Costa d'Or in southern Spain.

'Are you going to live there?' asked Harriet, when she recovered from the shock. She hadn't thought practical Emily would take her lightly spoken words seriously.

'No,' answered Emily smiling at her friend's stunned reaction, 'I couldn't leave England for good, my roots are too deep, but we'll spend the winter months in Spain. It will be good for

Beatrice's health, she really can't stand English winters for much longer and I can't say I enjoy them myself. I've put the house up for sale. It's much too big for us. It was when mother was alive, but she wouldn't move. We'll buy a little bungalow with a nice big garden. Beatrice is quite excited and so am I to be honest.'

Within six months, Emily was as good as her word. When she showed Harriet her letter of resignation, she said seriously: 'You must apply for my job, Harriet. You deserve some recognition for all you've done as my deputy. You're quite capable of taking over.'

When Harriet told Roger she was thinking of applying for Emily's job as Headmistress of Larkhill, he was not at all pleased.

'I suppose that will mean less time for us, with all the extra responsibility of a Headship,' was his immediate reaction.

'But more money,' replied Harriet seriously, 'and we'll need it if Zoe gets a

University place next year. Anyway, Roger, I've never neglected you or the children for my job, you know that.'

She was angry at Roger's attitude, and knew it came from resentment that she was able to support the family where he himself had failed.

And here she was, a year later, a year of hard work, worry and loneliness. Her appointment to Emily's job had been the last straw for Roger. When she told him he'd flown into a rage, for once in spite of the presence of Zoe and Ben.

'I can see I'm not needed now you're Madame High and Mighty. I can't take any more of playing second fiddle to you. I'm off.'

'No, Daddy,' whispered Zoe, 'you can't.'

'I'm sorry, poppet, but I must,' he replied, lowering his voice and putting an arm round his beloved daughter. 'Anyway, I've had the offer of a deal in Paris. I'm going to accept it tomorrow.'

Zoe pushed back her chair violently, they'd been having dinner, and stared at her mother, tears streaming down her face. The flash, almost of hatred, in her daughter's eyes, struck Harriet like a knife wound. Zoe shouted at her: 'Now look what you've done. I'll never forgive you, never!'

As Zoe rushed upstairs, Harriet caught a glimpse of Roger's face before he turned to follow his daughter. He was smiling, a glint of triumph in his eyes. At that moment Harriet despised him as she'd never done before.

Forcing back her own tears, she looked at her son. He, too, was staring at her, white-faced.

'You can't let him go, Mother!'

'But what can I do, Ben? He's got a deal in Paris.' Harriet couldn't hide the trace of sarcasm in her voice.

'You could refuse your promotion, then he'd stay.'

She looked down at the untouched food on her plate.

'And what then, Ben? He'll want me to give up my career altogether. He's always resented me working. If I give in to this . . . blackmail, there will be no end to it.'

'You make it sound like a war, Mother. Marriage isn't like that. It's give and take.' Newly-engaged Ben's voice was desperate. Harriet's heart went out to her son. She stretched across and touched his hands which were clenched tightly on the table.

'Ben, you must try to understand. This marriage, our marriage, isn't as perfect as you think it is. It hasn't been for a long time. It *is* like a war. Your father's right, it's got to end here or we'll destroy each other.'

Ben's eyes were uncomprehending: 'I'm sure all marriages have their bad patches, it can't be perfect all the time. But you could save it now if you really wanted to.'

Harriet felt a slow anger rise within her: 'You mean give up all I've worked for, had to work for, to send you both to University? We couldn't do it without me working. Your father . . . '

'Dad's had bad luck in his deals,'

interrupted Ben. 'Anyway, you don't work just for the money, or so you're always saying.'

'That's true, I enjoy my job and I wouldn't want to give it up now.'

'You see? You don't want to. Not even to stop our family from breaking up.'

Harriet sighed. How could he understand? She'd never told him. She'd always covered up for Roger. This deal in Paris, it would be just like all the others. His 'deals' were always expensive failures.

Slowly she rose to her feet and began to clear away the plates of untasted food. She felt Ben's eyes upon her, hurt and bewildered, and forced herself to ignore the plea in them.

As he left the room, she silently let the tears fall.

2

Harriet stirred restlessly on the lounger beside the pool. The sun was hot on her bare back. In one of her lately rare sunny moods, Zoe had persuaded her to get a couple of bikinis instead of the rather prim one-piece costumes she usually wore.

The quiet of the afternoon was suddenly shattered by the terrified scream of a young child not far away, which brought Harriet instinctively to her feet. Only stopping to fasten the back of her bikini top, she quickly peered round the villa complex. Most of the occupants of the other villas were either away or indoors enjoying their siesta, for there was no sign of the usual sun-worshippers round their pools.

Another frightened shriek brought her head round to the largest villa in the estate which was set somewhat apart on higher ground and screened by trees. She could see part of the large pool through the trees and a small head bobbing up and down in the turquoise-coloured water. The screams were coming from a child who appeared to have difficulty in keeping afloat.

Without bothering to find her wrap or sandals, Harriet quickly jumped over the low picket fence surrounding the Preston villa and raced across the grassy verges and gravel paths which separated the properties.

She opened the small gate into the large garden and regarded the scene before her, one not unfamiliar to a teacher of young children. Two very sunburned small boys wearing minute swimming trunks, obviously twins, were tantalizing the little girl who was trying to get out of the pool. The boys were beating the water with long bamboo poles every time she neared the edge and, panic-stricken, she dog-paddled to the centre of the pool which was almost certainly too deep for her to stand in.

Harriet jumped into the pool and waded to the centre. She picked up the frightened child, at the same time shouting in her most authorative voice. 'Stop that, you naughty boys. Put those sticks down this instant!'

The effect was electric. The boys dropped their poles and stared at her in astonishment and dismay.

The little girl, who was about five years old, clung to Harriet, sobbing loudly. Wading out of the pool, still holding the child, Harriet stood over the boys and regarded them fiercely. They were about eight years old with longish dark, curly hair and beautiful black velvety eyes.

'She could have drowned in there, didn't you realize?' Harriet said. They looked up at her uncomprehendingly and the little girl stopped crying. Slightly relaxing her arms, she stared solemnly into Harriet's face.

Realizing at once they couldn't understand, Harriet searched her memory for what little Spanish she knew.

' . . . Usted ninos . . . ' Lord, what was the Spanish word for naughty? She regarded the children, uncharacteristically at a loss as to how to deal with the situation, and the irony of it almost made her smile.

Keeping a severe look on her face with difficulty, she set down the little girl and picking up a towel which was lying on the terrazo paving near the pool, wiped the tears from the child's dusky cheek.

'Que occurre?' a deep voice questioned from behind Harriet's stooping figure.

She turned quickly to encounter a pair of black eyes, identical to those of the twin boys, in a face as darkly suntanned, but belonging to a man of about forty wearing an impeccable white suit and an expression of concern.

'I'm sorry, I don't speak Spanish very well,' apologized Harriet, suddenly aware of her near nakedness in the diminutive bikini.

The little girl saved the situation by bursting into tears again. She threw herself at the man, badly disfiguring his white suit with her wet body.

Disregarding his spoiled clothes he clasped the child in his arms and spoke quickly and softly to her in Spanish. She replied in the same language between sobs.

When the brief exchange was over, he looked sternly at the two boys who were still standing by the pool, and now appeared to be very frightened.

'Estoy muy disgustado!' Harriet was able to understand that he was very angry with the boys and angry he looked. She turned to leave as unobtrusively as she could but the Spaniard touched her arm to detain her.

'I apologize for the bad behaviour of my sons, Senora.' His English was perfect with only a slight accent. 'My daughter has told me what happened and that you came to rescue her. I'm afraid I was occupied on the telephone with a client from the United States.

The line was so faint that I closed my study door and didn't hear the children. The boys . . . ' he shrugged his shoulders in a Gallic gesture of comic despair.

'Boys will be boys,' replied Harriet mechanically. As she spoke she realised he was frankly staring at her half-exposed breasts in a way that brought the colour to her cheeks. Fervently wishing she'd brought a wrap with her she clasped her arms round her body in a purely defensive gesture.

At her movement he looked into her eyes in amused surprise which she found even more disturbing, making her heart beat faster.

'Please excuse me,' she said in as dignified a voice as she could manage. 'I can see I'm no longer needed. I must get back now.'

'But Senora, I haven't thanked you properly for helping my daughter. Please allow me to offer you a little refreshment. I'm sure Maria would like to thank you, too, now she has fully recovered.'

Indeed, little Maria, revelling in the attention, was smiling adorably at Harriet from the security of her father's arms. In spite of her embarrassment, Harriet returned the child's smile, noting again the beauty of her eyes and the extraordinarily long black eyelashes.

As if, at last, sensing Harriet's discomforture, the man bent down to pick up a large towel from one of the sun-beds on the terrace and bowing, handed it to her. Smiling gratefully, she fixed the towel round herself to cover as much of her body as she could and, hesitantly, followed him into the villa.

He motioned her towards a chair in the cool living room. At that moment, a woman wearing a white dress with a red belt and red sandals entered the room from another door. She was younger than Harriet and her shining dark hair was held in a thick chignon at the nape of her neck. Large dark brown eyes looked questioningly at the man and he handed the child to her with a brief explanation in Spanish. Her eyes went quickly to Harriet, then away, and she held Maria possessively close to her. He spoke again and she nodded, taking the child into another room, emerging almost immediately with a large pitcher of lemonade and two glasses, which she put down on a small table, pouring the cloudy liquid into the glasses, and then left the room.

'Now, allow me to introduce myself,' he said to Harriet when they were alone. 'I am Carlos Mendoza. You have met three of my children, Fernando, Pepe and Maria.' He looked questioningly at her.

'Harriet Maxwell,' she replied. 'I'm staying in the villa across the way, the one with the blue door and shutters.'

'Ah, the villa of the Misses Preston.'

'You know them?' Harriet was surprised, as Emily and Beatrice only used the villa during the winter months.

'Not well. When I am here we occasionally pass the time of day.' Senor Mendoza smiled: 'We spend most of our time here in the villa, winter and summer. Or at least the children do, with Consuela. My business is in Granada, but I travel a great deal. I come here as often as my business allows. I am a wine exporter.'

'You said just now I'd met some of your children. You have more?' queried Harriet with interest, sipping the cold refreshing lemonade.

'Oh, yes. I have a daughter, Carlotta. She is seventeen. She goes to a convent boarding school in Madrid. At present she is staying with a friend, but we hope to have her home here in a day or two.' He paused for a moment, then continued: 'The children's mother died two years ago, she was killed in a car accident.'

Harriet was shocked, as much by the cold, unemotional voice of the Spaniard, as by the sad information he had given. She'd taken it for granted that the dark Spanish woman, Consuela, was the children's mother. Certainly the woman's possessive attitude with the little girl gave that impression, as did the warmth of her expression as she looked at Carlos Mendoza. Harriet was suddenly aware that he was speaking again: 'After my wife's death I decided to sell our home in Granada and live here away from the hustle of the city. My wife didn't like it here — she preferred city life and all its attractions,' he concluded briefly.

'You have children?' he questioned.

She nodded. 'Yes, a boy and a girl. Zoe, my daughter, is staying here with me. She is seventeen, the same age as your daughter. Ben is five years older.' Harriet, like so many English people, could never get used to the very real interest many Continental people took in the private lives of others, even perfect strangers.

'And your husband? Is he with you?' pursued Carlos Mendoza.

'I'm awaiting the final decree of our divorce.' she answered briefly.

I'm sorry,' quietly, but he relentlessly went on with his questioning. 'And do you work? I understand many

Englishwomen have careers of their own.'

His voice seemed patronising to her over-sensitive ears and this was another question she was reluctant to answer. She had always been reticent about her job.

'I'm the Headmistress of a large Primary School in London's East End, in what is called a socially deprived area. Many of the children have very difficult home environments.' That ought to take the patronising smile from his face, she continued silently to herself.

But Carlos Mendoza's reaction was completely unexpected — utter hilarity. A delighted laugh burst from his lips as he regarded her with amusement.

Harriet was taken aback and a little offended.

'I see nothing funny . . . .' she began stiffly, rising as if to leave.

He stopped laughing immediately, restraining her with a hand on her shoulder.

'I must apologize for my seeming rudeness, Mrs. Maxwell. I didn't mean to offend you. But if you could see yourself at this moment — your words were hard to believe. I'm afraid I forgot my manners completely.'

She was again aware of her state of undress, although completely unconscious of the extremely attractive picture she made. In the towel-sarong, which exposed her beautiful shoulders and a great deal of her slender, well-shaped legs, the short, dark hair which curled softly round her flushed cheeks and the deep blue eyes, now sparkling with indignation and embarrassment, she looked more like a beautiful sixth-former caught playing truant from school, than the popular image of a stern headmistress.

Harriet failed to see the admiration which glowed in his dark eyes, but caught only the amusement on his sensuous lips. Hurriedly she said:

'I must go, my daughter will be returning for the evening meal.'

'Yes, of course. Oh!' he looked at her bare feet, 'you can't go home like that.' He went to the door leading to the kitchen and called imperiously in Spanish.

A moment later, Consuela emerged carrying a pair of espadrilles in her hands. She offered them to Harriet unsmilingly.

Harriet thanked her and Senor Mendoza said: 'Forgive me. This is Consuela, my late wife's cousin. Consuela looks after the children and runs the household. I don't know what we'd do without her,' he added casually. The woman smiled at him, her rather sombre face lightening and softening the perfect features with a sudden radiance which seemed to glow from within.

'She's in love with him,' thought Harriet with a faint pang of some emotion she'd not felt for many years. Could it be jealousy? She forced a friendly smile as Carlos Mendoza went on: 'Consuela, this is Mrs. Maxwell.

She is staying in the villa belonging to the Misses Preston.'

Consuela's gaze reluctantly turned to Harriet and Harriet's smile froze as she encountered the look of hostility on the face of the Spanish woman.

They walked to the gate and he held out his hand. 'Adios, Mrs. Maxwell. Thank you again for coming to my daughter's aid.'

3

The next morning, driving the small Seat car she'd hired for the holiday, Harriet went to Malaga, the nearest large town, to do some shopping.

As she wandered round the street market she heard a piping voice behind her: 'Senora!' Turning, she caught sight of the Mendoza child, Maria, excitedly pointing in her direction and trying to drag an obviously reluctant Consuela behind her. At last, impatiently dropping the Spanish woman's hand, Maria sped towards Harriet only to stop a few feet away, suddenly overcome by shyness.

'Buenas dias, Maria,' smiled Harriet then looked across at Consuela, who had just come abreast of the child. Harriet repeated her greeting to the stony-faced Spanish woman who, answering briefly and unsmilingly, firmly grasped the hand of the child and led her quickly through the crowds.

Finding herself disinclined to browse any further, Harriet left the market-place and made her way home, all thoughts of the occurrence disappearing when she found Ben and his fiancee had arrived.

'How lovely,' she cried, hugging Ben and kissing Gabrielle's coolly proffered cheek. 'We weren't expecting you until the week-end.' The girl's make-up was, as usual, immaculate, as was the rest of her elegant ensemble. All this after a two-day car journey through France and Spain.

'Yes, we managed to get away sooner,' said Ben.

'Did you have a good journey?' Harriet enquired as she poured them a drink.

'Grim!' answered Ben with a short laugh and Gabrielle, who'd up to then said little, gave him an angry glance.

Zoe, on hearing the voices, came running into the villa from the terrace and flung herself into her beloved brother's arms. 'How long are you staying?' she asked, after giving Gabrielle a markedly less enthusiastic welcome.

'A week or so,' Ben smiled at his young sister's exuberance. 'Gabrielle's doing an audition for a television advert next week and I've got an assignment in Scotland.' A journalist with a motoring magazine, Ben often tested new cars on the road.

'What's the advertisement for?' Harriet asked Gabrielle with interest.

Gabrielle unbent a little as she discussed her work: 'It's for a new shampoo. My agent thinks I've got a good chance of getting the contract. It would be nice to get into television, one way or another.'

Ben smiled at her proudly: 'With your hair, it's a cinch.' Indeed, Gabrielle had glorious dark-red tresses that reached almost to her waist. She usually wore it dressed in a chignon or twisted round her head, but today, in spite of the heat, it was loose and hung in long strands, waving slightly and curled at the ends. With her green, heavily lashed eyes and bright lipstick she made a striking picture.

Turning to Ben, Harriet thought he looked tired and strained and even Gabrielle's smooth, carefully composed face showed signs of tension.

Later, showing Gabrielle into Zoe's bedroom, she said: 'I hope you don't mind sharing with Zoe, Gabrielle, but we only have three bedrooms.' Gabrielle looked enquiringly at Ben, who frowned back at her. Pretending not to notice, Harriet went on: 'And your room's across the hall, Ben. I'll just show Gabrielle where everything is, then I'll come and show you around.'

She joined Ben and found him standing by the window, looking across the back garden of the villa where the swimming pool was situated.

'Sorry about Gabrielle having to share with Zoe, but the Misses Preston didn't think it was necessary to have more than three bedrooms. We're the only ones who use the villa apart from them. I don't think they anticipated we'd have such a crowd. And this room is very small . . . '

Ben smiled and coming towards her, put his arms round her as he used to in the old days: 'Mother, stop gabbling. It's alright.'

She looked up and met his eyes, so like her own, twinkling at her. He said: 'Honestly, Mum, I didn't expect anything different. Anyway, it's probably for the best, the way things are at the moment between Gabrielle and me.' Releasing her, he strode abruptly to the window.

'Do you want to talk about it, Ben?'

He shrugged his shoulders. 'I suppose it's my fault. I went into this like an adolescent thinking that because we loved each other everything would fall into place and we'd live happily ever after. That's why I was so upset about you and Dad. I didn't want to face the fact that sometimes things don't work out.'

Turning slowly to Harriet, he added, 'I'm sorry, Mum. I've been rotten to you lately. So has Zoe, but she's only a kid and I should have known better. But it *was* a shock y'know. You'd always seemed so happy together, the perfect couple everybody called you, and certainly Zoe and I thought so.'

'That was my fault,' said Harriet. She sat on the bed and looked into her son's troubled face. 'I felt I was doing the right thing, shielding you both from the quarrels, your father's excesses and weaknesses. For your own sakes I should have let you see things as they were.'

He came and sat beside her. 'I think I knew about Dad's weaknesses all the time and since you broke up I've begun to see things more clearly, remembering things I didn't want to recognise at the time. I remember hearing raised voices after we kids had gone to bed and listening to you crying. But, you see, in the mornings you'd be so cheerful and normal that

I'd think I'd been dreaming.'

He paused and looked at her searchingly. 'Dad told me he wants you to take him back. He said he'd been trying to persuade you. I think he's changed, Mum. He seems genuinely sorry and ready to make amends.'

Harriet sighed: 'Yes, I know, Ben. But it's too late.' One of the reasons she'd been so desperate to get away from London was to escape Roger's persistent phone calls and unexpected visits.

She changed the subject quickly. 'Enough of your father and me. Now tell me what the trouble is between Gabrielle and you?'

'I've already said too much. All I can really say is I'm beginning to have doubts. I don't know whether we're suited, although I still love her. But marriage ... frankly, Mum, I don't know.'

'Have you discussed this with Gabrielle?' Harriet asked gently.

'Of course I have, or tried to. But the more I express my doubts, the more keen she is to get married. When I was so anxious to get married straight after we got engaged, she kept putting it off. I shall never understand women!' disgustedly.

Harriet smiled: 'You probably never will if you're like ninety-nine percent of men.'

★   ★   ★

Over lunch Harriet mentioned the incident with the Mendoza children, although she didn't go into a great deal of detail, especially about her own mixed feelings towards Carlos Mendoza. They listened with interest, especially Zoe, who was eager to meet the daughter, Carlotta. This made it easy for Harriet to persuade her daughter to accompany her later that day in order to return the towel and the espadrilles loaned by Consuela.

Chiding herself for the need of moral support Harriet hastily put from her mind the sudden thought that it wasn't meeting the Spanish woman that bothered her, in her job she was quite able to handle difficult or obstructive people, but the memory of those teasing, all-seeing dark eyes of Carlos Mendoza . . .

All the same, she spent a great deal of care on her appearance and finally emerged wearing a pale yellow sundress with matching high-heeled sandals. Her dark, curly hair was flicked casually round her sun-tanned face and a pale lipstick was the only make-up she needed.

Ben and Zoe whistled in admiration when she appeared, and even Gabrielle showed appreciation. This brought a sparkle to her eyes making her feel ready for anything. Bring on Consuela and Carlos Mendoza, she silently challenged, but even the thought of his name made her pulses race.

'I wish Dad could see you now,' said Zoe as they walked along the gravel path towards the large villa.

'Whatever makes you say that?'

exclaimed Harriet. Zoe rarely mentioned her father nowadays, and at this particular moment Roger was the last person Harriet wanted to see or even think about.

'No real reason,' Zoe replied hastily, 'but he's still nuts about you.'

'What nonsense!' Harriet regarded her daughter's downcast face for a few moments, and, not stopping the brisk pace she'd set, said: 'You know, Zoe, you really must accept that there's nothing left between your father and me. It's all over — the final decree will be issued any day now.'

'There's still time for you to change your mind,' Zoe persisted.

'But I'm not going to, so let's say no more about it.' Harriet's voice was sharp.

Zoe looked at her mother from beneath her eyelashes. 'All right. But don't say I didn't warn you.'

With that cryptic remark hanging in the air between them, they arrived at the Mendoza villa. The door was

opened not by Consuela or her
employer, but by a slightly breathless
young girl wearing denim jeans and a
white tee-shirt. Huge black eyes,
fringed by impossibly long, curling
eyelashes stared at them shyly, and the
dark hair worn in a pony tail shone like
a raven's wing. The girl was unmistak-
ably a Mendoza and Harriet guessed it
must be Carlotta.

Harriet was the first to speak:
'Buenos dias, Senorita. Habla usted
ingles?' She fervently hoped the girl did
speak English, as she really didn't think
she could carry on a long conversation
in Spanish.

The girl smiled: 'Oh, yes. I speak
English a little.' Her voice was soft and
light and the slight Spanish accent was
very attractive.

'I am Harriet Maxwell and this is my
daughter Zoe. I . . . met your father and
brothers and sister yesterday. You are
Senorita Mendoza.'

'Yes I am Carlotta Mendoza. I am
very pleased to meet you. My father

told me how you helped my little sister yesterday.' By this time the girl had regained her composure as she opened the door wider. 'I was upstairs. I only arrived home an hour ago.'

'I'm sorry if we've come at an inconvenient time. We only called to return . . . '

'Oh, no, I didn't mean . . . ' Carlotta blushed furiously and Harriet, sympathising with the girl's obvious embarrassment, allowed herself and Zoe to be ushered into the sitting-room. 'Please sit down,' went on Carlotta, indicating the sofa where Harriet had sat the day before. 'My father will be very sorry to miss you. He had to take the children to the hospital.'

Harriet and Zoe stared at her in concern. She added hastily: 'It is not serious.' She smiled shyly at Harriet. 'You have met my brothers, Pepito and Fernandino.' The English woman nodded, noticing the affectionate use of the diminutive of the boys' names. Their sister went on: 'They are always rather naughty and they are always up to mischief. Not long after I arrived when I was talking to my father and Consuela about my holiday we heard the boys shouting from the garden. We found them at the top of a tree and Maria was with them. They were unable to get down and Maria was crying. She was very frightened. My father had to get a ladder and rescue them. He was very angry.'

'Were they hurt?' asked Harriet. 'You said your father had to take them to hospital.'

'Oh, no,' Carlotta laughed. 'They had slight scratches on their arms and legs and Consuela insisted they go to the hospital for injections against . . . how do you say it in English?'

'Tetanus?'

'Yes. Consuela is very fond of the children and concerns herself very much if they are hurt. My father told me you are . . . Headmistress? . . . of a school in England.' Adding as Harriet nodded .. 'My father said you were

severo . . . severe . . . with the boys ..
He said you must be a very good
Headmistress. They were quite fright-
ened.'

'Oh, I hope not,' said Harriet quickly,
'I was a little cross with them, but I
would hate them to be frightened of
me.'

'Well, just a little,' amended Carlotta,
obviously fearing she'd hurt her
guest's feelings. 'But my father was
very impressed. He said you were
formidable.' She grinned. 'He thinks
Consuela is too soft with them and
spoils them. He says they need a firmer
hand.'

She turned to Zoe and as the two
girls talked Harriet thought how charming the Spanish girl was. She would be
a good influence on Zoe, who was
inclined to be headstrong and a little
selfish. Suddenly Harriet felt that she
would like to get to know this lively
Spanish family better, or rather the
children, she hastily corrected herself.

Listening to the girls' conversation,

she discovered that although Carlotta appeared to be fairly emancipated, because of her jeans and tee-shirt, she was in fact quite restricted in her social life compared to English girls of the same age. Although she was seventeen and a half, she was not allowed to go out alone in the evenings, or even with her young friends. Zoe was too polite to show her surprise, but couldn't help asking Carlotta how she spent her time, especially when on holiday.

'I swim a lot and sunbathe in the garden. I meet my friends on the beach or in the town during the day. Sometimes in the evening we go, the whole family, to a restaurant where we meet family friends, or we visit each other's houses. There, we talk a lot, or someone sings or plays the piano. Usually though we spend the evening eating and talking.' Harriet thought, amused, that Zoe didn't appear very impressed by the girl's evening entertainment, and when the Spanish girl suddenly exclaimed: 'But you must come to dinner one evening! I will ask my father,' Zoe looked quickly at her mother in something like panic. Harriet grinned at her and murmured a polite acknowledgment to Carlotta.

A little later, Harriet stood up and said: 'We really must go now, Carlotta. Thank you very much for your hospitality. I do hope we'll see you again soon.'

Carlotta showed them to the door and just as they were stepping outside Harriet suddenly remembered the reason for their visit. 'Oh, I forgot. Please return these to Consuela with my thanks. It was very kind of her to lend them to me.' She handed Carlotta the espadrilles and towel and they went on their way.

As they walked slowly home, Zoe said: 'I hope they don't ask us to dinner. It sounds very boring. Carlotta said they sometimes take three or four hours to eat the meal.'

Harriet smiled: 'You'd probably enjoy it very much. They're very entertaining people and marvellous hosts, I under-stand. I think it would be most interesting.' However, she thought it very unlikely they'd be invited. Secretly she wasn't sure she could sit under Carlos' amused eyes for three or four hours. All the same she felt vaguely disappointed he hadn't been at home.

Zoe echoed her thoughts: 'It's a pity Carlotta's father and the maid weren't there today. I'm curious to meet them.'

'She's hardly a maid,' interjected Harriet.

'What is she then?'

'I don't really know. A relative of their mother, I believe Senor Mendoza said. She certainly doesn't dress like a maid!'

'Perhaps she's his mistress,' said Zoe casually over her shoulder as she turned in at the gate of their villa.

'It's none of our business what she is,' Harriet's voice was crisp. The same thought had occurred to her more than once, and she wondered why the idea was so repugnant. After all, what was he to Harriet? She'd only met him once. But the uneasy thought persisted in her mind.

4

A little later Harriet joined Zoe and sat down on one of the two loungers beside the pool. 'Pass the sun-tan oil, will you?' Zoe handed her the bottle and Harriet began to annoint her lightly tanned body. Ben and Gabrielle soon joined them, Ben in his swimming trunks and his fiancée wearing a cool, green linen dress and white high-heeled sandals. Her hair was covered by a chiffon scarf, topped by an elegant wide-brimmed sun-hat, and large round sunglasses almost completely hid the top half of her face. The carefully rouged mouth was set in a thin, straight line.

'Hello, you two,' greeted Ben. 'We've been into the village.' His voice was strained and his smile forced. It was obvious the engaged couple had been arguing, and Harriet quickly said:

'Come and sit under the umbrella, Gabrielle. The sun's still very hot.'

Gabrielle thanked her and without a glance at Ben sat on the canvas chair indicated by Harriet. 'What have you been doing in the village?' asked Harriet brightly to cover the sudden heavy silence.

'Oh, just looking round the shops and then we went for a drink,' Ben answered. He was lying on the terrace, a towel beneath his body and his head pillowed on his arms.

'And Ben was bored,' added Gabrielle in a tight voice. Ben said nothing.

Zoe asked: 'D'you like Mum's new swimsuit? She bought it in Malaga this morning.'

Gabrielle switched her gaze to Harriet who was now stretched on her back in the sun and said sincerely: 'It really is lovely! I've not been to Malaga. We must go one day. The shops aren't much good in the village, of course, but it's quite pretty there.'

The women talked about clothes for

a while, until suddenly Ben got up, dived into the pool and began to swim energetically up and down. Zoe gave a whoop and quickly getting to her feet dived in after him, trying to catch up with his strong strokes. Gabrielle watched them, her eyes troubled.

'Is there anything wrong?' ventured Harriet, turning to face the girl. She knew she was risking a snub but felt she couldn't ignore the situation.

For a few minutes Gabrielle didn't answer, then: 'I shouldn't have come. This isn't my sort of holiday at all, but I thought it might do us good to get away together. It's been a horrible mistake though.'

'It's early yet, you've only been here for one day.'

'We've done nothing but argue ever since we left London. The journey was a nightmare.' Gabrielle's eyes suddenly filled with tears.

'Perhaps it would help to talk — if you want to,' Harriet put her hand on the girl's arm. This was a Gabrielle she did not recognise — vulnerable and unhappy.

Fumbling for a handkerchief, Gabrielle surreptitiously dabbed at her eyes. 'Ben and I are so different,' she said at last. 'I knew that from the beginning. So did he, but he insisted it didn't matter. At first he always did what I wanted and, to be honest, I let him. Unfortunately, because of the nature of our work, we models receive a great deal of flattery and attention. It was like that for me, anyway, and, well, I took it for granted. I used to treat Ben very badly, but I did love him — I do love him,' she corrected. 'He is so unlike the other men I'd known, so calm and easy-going, but dependable. I always felt secure with him. But now . . . ' she sighed.

'But now . . . ' prompted Harriet gently.

'He's changed. He's restless and irritable — doesn't like going to our usual places. Says smart restaurants and discos bore him, my friends bore him.

In fact. I think that *I* bore him. That's why I thought a change of scene might do us good, but it only seems to widen the gap between us. I'm so out of place here.'

'What are the differences between you? Most couples have different likes and dislikes — that's often what makes the relationship interesting.' Harriet felt she wanted to help the girl and realized with a sense of shame she hardly knew her, and had made little attempt to remedy the situation before. All her training and experience had taught her not to judge people from the outside and she'd broken the golden rule with her own son's fiancée. She tried to excuse herself! 'It's so difficult to be impartial when people you love are concerned.'

Gabrielle was watching Ben and his sister ducking each other in the pool. They were shrieking with laughter and demonstrating the water skills they'd learnt at an early age.

'That's one difference,' she remarked,

nodding towards the two in the pool.

'Can't you swim? That's easily remedied. Why don't you ask Ben to teach you?'

'That's only part of it. I was always hopeless at games at school. I made no end of excuses to get out of doing them. I think the teachers gave up on me in the end and didn't bother.' She laughed ruefully. 'You know how Ben loves football, cricket, golf, tennis, swimming. He used to ask me to go with him when we first got engaged, but I didn't really understand what was going on and Ben thought I was bored so he stopped asking me. He said I was the indoor type. It used to amuse him, but now he seems to resent it.'

'But many couples are like that,' protested Harriet. 'In fact it was the opposite with Roger and me. I was the sporty one and he was the indoor type.' She stopped suddenly, aware of the tactlessness of her remark. Gabrielle raised a half-humorous eyebrow at Harriet, who quickly said: 'I'm sorry, that was a bit tasteless, wasn't it? The obvious answer to that one is look where Roger and I are now. But there was a great deal more to our break-up than a game of tennis.'

'I'm sure there was, but it illustrates what could happen and, to be honest, that's what I'm afraid of now.' Gabrielle swallowed. 'I couldn't bear to lose Ben, Harriet.'

As Harriet looked into the girl's tear-filled eyes, she saw the sincerity shining there and was deeply moved.

'Well, we'll have to make sure you don't, won't we?' she said briskly.

Gabrielle wiped her eyes with the back of her hand and Harriet remarked with a grin, 'That's a good start.'

'What is?' asked Gabrielle, surprised.

'You've lost one of your false eyelashes.'

'Oh, God, where?' the girl leapt to her feet and proceeded to search the ground.

'Relax,' laughing, Harriet stretched out her hand and retrieved the offending set of eyelashes from a strand of Gabrielle's long red tresses, now escaping the restricting headscarf.

As she handed the spider-like lashes over, Harriet said on impulse: 'Why don't you get into a swimsuit and sunbathe?' At Gabrielle's look of horror, she added: 'Oh, do you burn? Your skin *is* very fair.'

The girl answered with a shamefaced smile: 'I don't even own a swimsuit. As for sun-bathing, I don't know if I'd burn, I've never tried. My mother would never let me when I was small — she didn't want me to spoil my complexion.' She paused, then: 'You didn't meet my mother. Neither did Ben, she died about two years before I met him. You know, she once told me that on the day I was born she decided I'd be a film actress and she raised me with that one thought in mind.'

Harriet looked horrified.

'Yes,' said Gabrielle, averting her face, 'she was devastated when I showed no talent for acting, even though that probably wouldn't have mattered very much. Anyway, she changed her mind and decided I should be a model instead. A top model — *the* top model.'

'How old were you then?'

'About seven, I think.'

Harriet nodded, she knew of many such parents who, disappointed at their own lack of success, moulded their children from an early age to do what they themselves had either failed or had no opportunity to do. Feeling desperately sorry for Gabrielle, she asked: 'But what's that got to do with sun-bathing now? Sun-tanned beauties are the fashion.'

'But I'm no beauty,' said Gabrielle with no trace of false modesty, 'I never have been. I'm a type. Underneath all this make-up I'm very ordinary looking. All I have is my rather unusual colouring. Red hair, green eyes, pale, pale skin. It's quite rare nowadays and my mother was very forseeing. She managed to get me modelling jobs even when I was quite young — complexion creams, soaps — in fact my pale skin has been the reason for my success and will probably continue to be. Do you know, Harriet, it's even written in my contract that I mustn't get my face even faintly sun-tanned! If I break my contract, my career would be finished. All that I've worked for, and my mother lived for, would be wasted. This make-up is as much for protection from the sun as for decoration.'

There was a note of desperation in her voice: 'Take off my make-up, my lipstick, blusher, cut my hair short and you wouldn't know me. What's worse, nor would Ben!'

'You mean,' said Harriet in amazement, 'that Ben's never seen you . . . '

' . . . without make-up?' finished the girl for her. 'No. Even when . . . ' she stopped and looked embarrassed, then went on steadily, 'when he's with me I get up early and renew my make-up, so he'd always see me at my best. I don't want to disillusion him.' She attempted a light laugh, but it sounded more like a sob.

'D'you think you're being fair?' Harriet asked gently. 'If Ben really loves you, he loves you for yourself, not your looks.'

'I couldn't risk it before, and now . . . well, I'm beginning to think that Ben did fall just for my looks, my success, my glamorous image.'

'Nonsense,' declared Harriet, but from what both Ben and Gabrielle had told her she was beginning to wonder if the girl might be right. She knew from her own experience how easy it was to become infatuated with a person without really knowing him, or her. She'd fallen in love with Roger because he was handsome, witty, seemingly successful. She'd ignored the early warning signals, his quick temper, flirtatiousness and carelessness with money, thinking that love was all that mattered. Hadn't Ben said almost the same thing this morning?

'Perhaps it's time you began to find out what you really want from life,' Harriet went on carefully.

Gabrielle looked up at her: 'What do you mean?'

'Do you enjoy your present life-style?'

Gabrielle thought hard for a moment. 'It's all I know,' she answered at last. 'To be honest I enjoy the flattery and attention, what girl doesn't. But sometimes, in fact more so since I've known Ben, I think it's a bit phoney, and there must be more to life.' She looked again at the couple frolicking in the water. 'I feel I've missed out on being young and carefree. I wish it wasn't so important what I look like all the time.'

'But you can change that,' said Harriet. Gabrielle laughed a little bitterly. 'It's second nature to me. Look what happened when I lost my eyelashes. I nearly had a seizure. It's not easy changing when you've been conditioned for as long as I have.'

Harriet continued her train of thought, half to herself: 'It seems to me that you may *have* to choose.'

The girl was startled. 'You mean choose between Ben and my modelling?'

Harriet nodded. 'It depends how much you want Ben. Because if, as you say, Ben does only love you for your image, and I sincerely hope you're wrong, it won't last. You can't hide behind your make-up for ever. What about when you're married. You won't feel like getting up early every morning to do your face. Be practical, Gabrielle, if you leave it until you're married Ben will feel you've deceived him and he'll never forgive you. Anyway,' she added comfortingly, 'I think you may be unduly pessimistic about your modelling. I still think you could make a good career of it even if you did risk breaking your present contract.. You have other assets, a good figure, your lovely hair and eyes.'

Gabrielle was thoughtful: 'You realize I could end up with nothing, no Ben, no career.'

'That's why I said find out what you really want from life. Unless you're absolutely sure about your own feelings for Ben, you may find the risk too great. I'm sorry, Gabrielle,' said Harriet, sadly, 'I can't offer any magic formula to make it all right. Life's not like that. You've got to risk happiness to find it.'

Before the girl could say anything, they were interrupted by Ben and Zoe, laughing and wrestling and shaking water all over the terrace floor. Zoe flopped down beside the other two women and Ben, picking up a towel began to rub his hair vigorously.

'What are you two looking so serious about?' he asked, peering through the ends of the towel.

'Oh — women's talk,' answered Harriet, smiling with forced cheerfulness.

Gabrielle stood up. 'I'm going to

have a shower before dinner. I shan't be long.' She suddenly bent down and kissed Harriet on the cheek. 'Thanks, Harriet.'

5

Over breakfast the next morning, Ben suggested a visit to one of the more secluded beaches further along the coast. Zoe was enthusiastic as usual, but Harriet said she'd stay in the villa to catch up on the chores. Also she had to write to Emily who'd be wondering how they were getting on and if everything was satisfactory.

Gabrielle looked at Ben and said quietly: 'D'you mind if I don't come, Ben? I've got a bit of a headache and I'd rather stay here, if Harriet doesn't mind.' Indeed she did look paler than usual and there were dark shadows under her eyes as if she hadn't slept very well.

Ben regarded her anxiously, but managed to look like a disappointed small boy. 'Are you sure? Would you like me to stay with you?'

'No, you go with Zoe, I won't be much company for you.' When he still looked hesitant in spite of Zoe tugging on his arm, Gabrielle insisted. Rather too firmly, Harriet thought.

'Well, if you're sure,' he said finally and the two young Maxwells went upstairs to get their swimming gear.

'Are you all right?' asked Harriet in concern.

Gabrielle smiled palely at her. 'Yes, thanks. I really have got a bit of a headache. It'll soon go. Are you using your car today?'

'I was going to the market for some vegetables in a little while. Why?'

'I rather wondered if I could borrow it? I could get any shopping you want. I thought of going to Malaga.'

Gabrielle sounded mysterious and Harriet said: 'If you're going all that way would you like me to come too?'

'I'd rather like to go on my own if you don't mind. I've been thinking about what you said and I hardly slept last night, but there's still some more things I'd like to sort out.'

Harriet agreed, still feeling rather curious, and half-an-hour later Gabrielle expertly manoeuvred the Seat out of the drive. Harriet sat on the terrace writing to Emily.

'Good morning, Mrs. Maxwell.' The deep voice roused her from her writing and she looked up in amazement at the dark, handsome figure of Carlos Mendoza. He was smiling down at her: 'I knocked at your door several times, then I noticed your car wasn't in the drive. I decided you must be out but on an impulse walked round here just to make sure. I'm glad I did.' The look in his black eyes was enough to make Harriet thankful that, this time, she was well covered by her full-length kaftan. Only her narrow, well-shaped feet with the newly-painted toenails peeped from beneath.

'Why, oh, why does he have this effect on me?' she thought. Pulling herself together, she smiled back and said: 'Would you like to sit down?' and motioned to the canvas chair next to her lounger.

'Thank you. My daughter told me about your visit yesterday. I'm sorry I was out. She and your daughter seemed to get on very well.'

'Yes, they're about the same age, but very unalike in temperament, I think. However, they have a lot in common. I hope they become friends.'

'Carlotta is shy with strangers, but she is quite lively when she feels at ease.'

'I'm afraid Zoe is a little spoilt. It's partly my fault. She was very upset when my husband and I separated. He doted on her and I've been too soft with her since he went. She really needs a firmer hand.' Harriet sighed.

'I'm surprised to hear you say that. I thought how firm and authoritative you were with my sons the other day.' 'Formidable', corrected Harriet silently.

'I think it is true to say that teachers are often not the best parents,' she said thoughtfully. 'They are too emotionally involved. I can deal with other people's children far more easily than my own.'

'Was it Zoe you were worrying about when I interrupted you just now?' he asked suddenly.

She looked at him in surprise. 'How did you know I was worrying?' she asked.

He laughed: 'You had a mother-hen brooding look on your face.'

She laughed with him, her antagonism suddenly disappearing. 'Would you like some coffee?' she asked. 'I usually have some at this time. That is, of course, if you're not in a hurry to go?'

'I'm in no hurry,' he answered. Indeed he looked quite at home, leaning back in the canvas chair with his cheroot dangling from the strong brown fingers.

Harriet rose from the lounger and went towards the kitchen. He got up from his chair and followed her, perching on the corner of the kitchen table while she busied herself measuring coffee into the percolator.

'What were you worrying about?' His voice was gentle, the teasing note gone. She felt confused by the varying emotions he roused in her.

'Oh, my son and his fiancée are having some problems.' Harriet answered slowly.

'And you're sorting them out, I expect,' he said, still in that gentle voice.

'No, not really. But I can't help being concerned for them. They're so young.'

Carlos laughed again, this time the teasing note was back. 'And you're so old and experienced.'

'I don't want them to make the same mistakes as I did. It can be very painful.' Finding he was looking at her searchingly, she turned to the bubbling percolator and lifted it from the stove.

The coffee ready on a tray, he picked it up and they went back to the terrace.

'Actually,' he said, 'I came to invite you and your family to dinner at the villa on Friday night.

'That's very kind of you,' she answered. 'Thank you. I can't really speak for the others, but I'm sure they'll be delighted. Can I let you know later?' She was grateful to him for not pursuing their conversation in the kitchen. Like Emily, he seemed to be the type of person you could say anything to and he'd understand. She hardly knew him, though in a strange way she felt she'd known him for a long time.

They talked generally while drinking their coffee — about their children, books they'd both read and enjoyed. She discovered he was a great lover of England and the English way of life, having lived there for several years when he was very young. His English was excellent, apart from the faint accent, which, like his daughter's, was extremely attractive.

Harriet told him about her job, her friend Emily's help and guidance, relating the problems she had to deal with, not only educational but social, as the area around the school was occupied by families with problems — poverty, vandalism and broken homes, which reflected on the children's behaviour and attitude towards learning.

She learned from Carlos that he travelled a great deal in his business, to England, France and other European countries as well as the United States.

'I know very little about wine except that I like some and dislike others,' she confessed ruefully.

'We'll have to remedy that,' Carlos answered with a teasing smile. Embarrassed by the look in his eyes, she changed the subject quickly, asking tentatively about his wife's accident.

His eyes lost their teasing look and became bleak. After a small silence, he said shortly: 'She was in a car with another man. They'd been to a night club — it was late — they'd been drinking. The car went into a tree. They were both killed instantly.' So much was not said in those few brief sentences that Harriet found it difficult to speak.

'I'm sorry,' she said at last. 'I shouldn't have . . . '

'No, it's alright.' He looked at her almost in surprise. 'I've not talked to anyone about the circumstances of the accident before.' His laugh this time was bitter. 'I preferred to put it out of my mind.'

'I didn't mean to pry . . . ' Harriet was uncomfortable.

'You're a good listener, Mrs. Maxwell. May I call you Harriet?' She smilingly nodded agreement. He went on: 'I feel as if I've known you for a long time. I'll have to be careful or I'll tell you *all* my secrets. It's easy to see why the parents of your children at school come to you with their problems.' Once more his smile was warm, friendly.

'Roger, my husband, was a great talker . . . ' She stopped, suddenly unwilling to bring Roger into the intimate atmosphere which seemed to have grown between her and the Spaniard.

'Yes?' queried Carlos.

'Oh, nothing really. I was going to say that's probably where I received my first lessons in listening. He wasn't interested in my thoughts and dreams — they weren't very interesting anyway, except to me. So I listened to him, until I realised he had nothing to say . . . and I stopped listening.' She sighed, remembering.

After a small, comfortable silence, Carlos said softly: 'I'd like to hear about your thoughts and dreams sometime, Harriet.'

Startled, her eyes met his. They looked at each other for a long time, Harriet found she couldn't tear her eyes from his. Her heart began to race. Carlos leaned towards her . . .

At that moment, the car pulled up at the drive and Zoe and Ben tumbled out, arguing boisterously as usual. They stopped in surprise when they saw their mother's visitor.

Struggling for composure, Harriet introduced her children to Carlos, who kissed Zoe's hand to her obvious delight and shook Ben's hand warmly. 'I was just leaving, I didn't realise it was so late,' he said. He repeated his invitation to dinner and Harriet was amused to see Zoe's thrilled reaction, after her daughter's comment when coming away from the villa the day before.

When he'd at last taken his leave, Zoe drew an exaggerated deep breath and said to her mother: 'You didn't tell us what a dish Carlotta's father is. When he kissed my hand I went weak at the knees.'

'Not you too,' thought her mother rather sourly, but she smiled at Zoe's enraptured expression. She, herself, was beginning to feel a strong reaction to Carlos' visit and suddenly wanted to be alone to examine the strange feelings and yearnings she thought had died in her long ago, but now awakened by the handsome Spaniard. She excused herself before getting involved in further conversation about Carlos and was walking towards the door when the Seat drew up alongside Ben's car in the driveway.

Zoe's cry of surprise brought her to a halt and she turned reluctantly to see a transformed Gabrielle climb self-consciously out of the car. Harriet's smile froze on her face. Gabrielle had been right when she said how different she'd look without her 'trappings'. Gone were the long, thick tresses and heavy makeup. Apart from a pale brownish-coloured lipstick and light foundation, her face was devoid of cosmetics. Her hair was now very short and resembled a shining bronze cap, expertly cut close to her shapely head and feathering lightly round the finely sculptured face. She looked extremely pretty, but of the Gabrielle they all knew there was no trace.

Harriet went towards her and kissed her. 'You look wonderful!' she exclaimed in all sincerity. Zoe echoed her admiringly, but Ben was ominously silent.

'Let him like it,' Harriet prayed as the girl stood uncertainly in front of her stony-faced fiancé.

'What do you think, Ben?' Gabrielle asked in a small voice.

Suddenly he took her by the arms and shook her: 'What the hell have you done to yourself?' His voice was harsh.

'You're hurting me.' She pulled herself away from him, the tears beginning to flow.

Ben visibly pulled himself together. His voice lost some of its harshness. 'Well,' he asked. 'What's this all about?'

'I decided to change my image. I felt uncomfortable — overdressed. My hair was too heavy and making my head ache in this heat.' Gabrielle sobbed.

'What about the audition next week for that shampoo advert? You can't do that with short hair.'

'That's all you care about. My modelling and all it stands for.' Gabrielle stopped crying and turned angrily away from him. As she walked towards the villa she said quietly to Harriet, who with Zoe had been watching the couple in concern: 'You see, Harriet. I was right.'

'That was unforgivable, Ben,' said his mother furiously.

He took a deep breath. 'I know, Mother.' He rubbed his hands over his hair, still unruly from swimming in the sea earlier in the day. 'It was such a shock. She must be crazy.'

'I'm sure she has her reasons,' Harriet said coldly. 'Why don't you go and talk to her? She's very hurt. How could you be so unfeeling?'

Ben's face was sullen. 'Not now. I'll only upset her more. I need a drink.' He went indoors and returned with a glass of whisky in his hand, sitting down on the chair so recently vacated by Carlos Mendoza.

Harriet sat in the chair next to him, closing her eyes wearily, while Zoe stretched out on the lounger.

'I rather liked your Senor Mendoza,'

said Ben after a long silence, obviously trying to ease the tension in the atmosphere.

'He's not *mine*,' answered Harriet emphatically.

'Well, I think he'd like to be, the way he was looking at you,' teased Ben.

Harriet said quickly: 'Don't be silly,' a deep blush rising on her face in her consternation.

'Yes, Ben, don't be silly.' Zoe's voice was cold. She looked at her mother's confusion calculatingly. 'Mum's much too old for him.'

The cruelty in her daughter's words — and the truth — struck Harriet like a douche of cold water. She rose quickly and picking up the tray of dirty coffee cups walked blindly towards the kitchen, vaguely hearing Ben's angry admonition of his sister, and her sulky reply.

'It *is* true,' she thought bitterly. 'I must be older than he is.' She put the tray on the draining board and, holding on to the sink edge as if for support, stared out of the window, not seeing the beauty of the landscape before her. 'Why did this have to happen to me?'

When Zoe joined her Harriet was peeling the potatoes she was preparing for lunch rather more forcibly than was necessary. She reached in the 'fridge and handed a wrapped lettuce to Zoe. 'Wash the lettuce, please, then go and tell Gabrielle that lunch is nearly ready. I'm just going to put the steaks under the grill.'

'Ben's gone up to see her,' Zoe replied, 'I think that's them now.'

Ben and Gabrielle appeared, holding hands, but neither looking very happy.

The meal was a rather quiet affair, each person occupied with his or her own thoughts. Occasionally Zoe broke the silence, only to put forward further argument on why older men were so much more attractive than young boys, or how handsome Spanish men were, although no-one could be bothered to argue. Harriet was relieved when Ben offered to help her wash up while the girls went upstairs to decide on something for Zoe to wear to the dinner in two days' time. Gabrielle had, to the young girl's delight, offered to lend her one of her numerous dresses. 'Have you sorted things out with Gabrielle?' Harriet asked Ben as he was thoughtfully wiping a plate.

'So-so. It's just I don't know where I am at the moment. It's not only the hair-style and all that, but Gabrielle herself. She's different and I'm not sure if I like the change.' He sounded confused.

'You'll get used to it,' said his mother hopefully.

'Perhaps. It's funny, — though. I was only saying to you yesterday how uncertain I was about our relationship — and that was before all this happened. I was getting fed up with the jet-setting life she likes to lead, wondering if I'd ever really fit in. But that's Gabrielle, that's what I fell for. She seemed so glamorous and I couldn't believe she could actually love me too. You should see some of the types she used to go around with, sophisticated, rich, men of the world. I was really knocked out!' He grinned ruefully. 'I was almost afraid to kiss her at first.'

'I think the trouble with you, Ben,' said Harriet, 'is that you put women on a pedestal. You forget that we're human too and have our little failings, just like men. Look how upset you were when your father and I split up.'

'You may be right,' he answered slowly. He began putting the plates he'd dried on the cabinet shelf. 'But where does that leave me with Gabrielle?'

'Give it time. You know, she's just as confused and unhappy as you are. You've not been much help to her, especially today. I'm sorry to have to say this, Ben, but I think you'll just have to grow up — quickly.'

Ben looked at his mother in surprise. She didn't often criticize him, especially lately, when they hadn't been as close and she'd seemed to let him go his own way. He'd missed that, her wise and loving comments which, even if lightly given always made him take stock of the situation.

Now she looked back at him, rather sadly. It wasn't going to be easy, for either Ben or Gabrielle. Anyway, she'd had her say, now they must find their own solution.

6

Over breakfast the family discussed their plans for the day. Ben and Zoe wanted to go to the beach as usual. Gabrielle had astonished everyone by accompanying them yesterday sporting a new bikini and lashings of protective sun creams.

In spite of this precaution and carefully timed exposure to the sun's rays, poor Gabrielle had become pinkly and painfully sunburnt. She was mortified, Ben horrified, Zoe and Harriet sympathetic. Reluctantly she decided to stay out of the sun today. Reluctantly, because to her surprise she found she enjoyed the day on the beach and had joined in the frolicking with Ben and Zoe in the sea. This, of course, was where the damage was done as the sun's reflected rays from the sea were even more intense than on the beach.

Harriet was impressed by the girl's determination, but thought Ben was more embarrassed than flattered. He was used to a 'perfect' Gabrielle and this pink, rather awkward figure, unused to athletic games, unsettled him. It was like taking a rare tropical flower away from its proper environment.

*　*　*

Ben was proud of the three women as he escorted them to the Mendoza villa that evening.

Carlos was, as usual, looking magnificent, this time wearing a white dinner jacket, and he and Carlotta, who was simply but beautifully dressed also in white, greeted the Maxwells on the terrace. Harriet had felt shy on meeting Carlos again, but he, after taking her shawl and raising his eyebrows teasingly at her plunging neckline, politely kissed her hand and moved on to the younger girls. A little piqued at what she felt to be a rather casual greeting, she moved across to Carlotta who was talking to Ben. He was holding her shapely hand and smiling into her beautiful dark eyes. Carlotta was shyly laughing at what he was saying in his passable Spanish. Harriet thought with a faint tinge of alarm that they looked extremely well together.

Obviously, Gabrielle had the same thought as she called Ben to her side after being greeted by Carlos. Ben reluctantly tore his eyes from the Spanish girl's bewitching face and joined the other group as they moved towards the chairs set round a table laden with drinks beside the swimming pool.

Beginning to feel that the long-awaited evening was going to be somewhat of an ordeal, Harriet sipped her drink and smiled politely at Carlos' frank admiration of the women's dresses. The sudden appearance of Consuela at the table, flamboyantly but stunningly dressed in a red flamenco-style ensemble, did little to raise Harriet's spirits. The Spanish woman apologized charmingly in broken English for not appearing before to greet them. She was busy, she told them, looking after the kitchen staff hired for the evening to help her. The dinner was now ready, she went on, and would they please follow her?

Consuela directed the guests to their seats and took the chair opposite Carlos who seated himself at the head of the rectangular table. Harriet had assumed that Carlotta, as the daughter of the household would be hostess on such an occasion. The sight of Consuela obviously well-used to the role, made Harriet revise her opinion of her importance in the family.

The meal was sumptuous, the main course being paella, although Harriet barely noticed what she was eating. Conscious of Ben's admiring glances and whispered comments to Carlotta with whom he was sitting, Gabrielle's misery, isolated across the table seated next to Zoe, whose flirtatiousness with Carlos was warmly and gallantly reciprocated and Consuela's darkly triumphant glances towards herself, Harriet wished she was anywhere but at this table, in this house.

Harriet ate little, but sipped nervously at her wine, not noticing that the glass was always full, thanks to Carlos' discreet attentiveness. They were all by this time on first name terms, except that Consuela, on the few occasions she addressed Harriet directly, insisted on calling her Mrs. Maxwell in a manner that was far from polite or respectful. At one stage, Carlos sharply corrected her, whereupon the Spanish woman shrugged her shoulders and refrained from addressing Harriet at all.

When eventually it was time to go, Harriet went through the motions, her head feeling strangely light and her legs water-filled. Controlling her actions and speech with iron determination, she was glad to see that no-one appeared to notice her slight tipsiness.

Turning to leave the villa, she clutched Ben's free arm and made a dignified exit.

Zoe chattered brightly as they walked back to the villa, obviously enraptured by the attentions paid to her by their host, but her companions were silent, immersed in their own thoughts.

After saying goodnight and shakily climbing the stairs, Harriet collapsed into the arm-chair in her bedroom. She covered her face in her hands and wept silently — part relief for the end of such a long, depressing evening and part mortification at her own carelessness in drinking too much wine.

Suddenly she heard a sharp sound on the half-closed shutters and, startled, went to the window.

Carlos was standing in the moonlight looking up at her. Opening the shutters wider, she leaned out and demanded in a loud whisper: 'What on earth are you doing?'

'Throwing stones at your window,' was the audacious reply and she could just discern in the darkness a mischievous grin on his face, reminiscent of one of his young sons: 'Come down here. I want to talk to you.'

'I can't,' she hissed back. 'Do you know what time it is?'

'Yes, it's late. Come down.'

'I really can't,' suddenly thinking of the stairs she'd have to descend in the process. And she was much too tired to hide how tipsy she was feeling.

'Why not? Come on, you need some fresh air in your state.'

She caught her breath: 'What state?' Her voice was indignant, embarrassment flooding over her at the realization that he'd known all the time.

'You've had too much wine and too little to eat tonight. A walk will do you good.'

She stared at him for a minute in silence then, knowing she'd not sleep if she went to bed and that he was right about the fresh air, she nodded briefly: 'All right. I won't be a minute.'

Picking up her white shawl, she

carefully and silently descended the wide staircase and went out to the terrace. Carlos was beside her in seconds. Taking the shawl from her nerveless fingers, he put it round her shoulders and led her to the car he'd parked a little way from the entrance to the villa.

'I thought you said we were going for a walk,' she said as she climbed into the passenger seat.

'We are,' answered Carlos, walking round the car, 'but first we've got to get there.'

'Where?'

'You'll see,' was the enigmatic reply and Harriet had a moment of hysteria. Where was he taking her? Was she dreaming? Suddenly she didn't care and rested her head against the back of the seat, stretching her legs out in front of her.

'That's better,' said Carlos approvingly. 'Now you're beginning to relax at last. You know, Harriet, when you're away from your family you're a different person.'

'How different?' Harriet's eyes were closed and her voice was drowsy, the faint drone of the car's engine almost lulling her to sleep.

'More yourself. When you're with them you're worrying about them, what they're doing, whether they're unhappy. Think about yourself now and forget them. They're old enough to be in charge of their own destinies.'

'Yes, I know,' she murmured. There was a small, comfortable silence. 'It was very pleasant tonight, wasn't it?' she remarked sleepily.

'Don't be hypocritical. You had a terrible time. I had to keep filling your wine-glass to try and get you relaxed.'

She opened her eyes suddenly and looked at him. His teeth flashed white in the semi-darkness of the car. 'You mean . . . you made me drunk on purpose?'

'Not at all. Relaxed I said.'

'I feel very ashamed of myself,' Harriet closed her eyes again. 'I don't usually drink too much, you know.'

'I'm sure you don't, but I must say you looked very sweet trying to walk steadily from my villa.' She knew from the teasing inflection in his voice he was laughing at her again, but she was too comfortable and sleepy to be annoyed. In fact, she was beginning to see the funny side herself.

She giggled softly to herself. Carlos's hand brushed against her leg as he changed gear to negotiate a tight bend in the road and Harriet felt a delicious thrill run through her body at the contact. She asked, her breath catching: 'Are you going to seduce me now?'

'Harriet! The thought never crossed my mind.' His voice was shocked but the look in his eyes belied the words.

Harriet sat up swiftly, instantly wide awake: 'You see what wine does to me. It makes me say dreadful things. I'm really not like this at all.'

Carlos turned the car off the road and drove over a short, rough track towards a small, sandy beach. Pulling

97

up the handbrake and switching off the engine he turned to her: 'Well, do you like it?'

She was looking at him but now she looked around: 'Carlos, it's beautiful. I didn't know this beach existed.'

'Not many people do. That's why our family comes here. It never gets crowded, even in the height of summer. Shall we walk?'

He got out and came to open the door, holding out his hand to help her. Clasping the shawl round her shoulders against the slight, cool breeze, she took his hand and let him guide her down to the little sandy cove, sheltered by the rocks and trees making it both private and free from adverse winds.

Harriet was the first to speak as they went slowly along the shore.

'What did you mean when you said I wasn't myself when I'm with my family? How can you know what I'm really like?'

'I don't know, but I can guess. I meant that you always seem to be hiding behind a different face — your mother-hen face, your school teacher face, your social face. I know,' he added, correctly anticipating her, 'that everybody uses a different manner to suit the occasion sometimes, but you use your 'faces' as a shield, to hide behind, as though you're afraid to let people know the real you. I keep having tantalizing glimpses.' He laughed softly. 'You know on the day we met when you were with the children. I was watching you for a few minutes before I interrupted, but your manner changed with me. I think the only time you're really natural is when you're with children — or drunk.' Harriet gasped. He turned her to face him and his eyes were soft and tender. 'It's true — on those occasions you let your defences down. Like now.'

He bent his head and kissed her gently on the lips. After the first second of shock, Harriet felt the warmth of his lips and the tenderness behind his kiss. She responded shyly at first, then with equal warmth as his arms went round her. Her own arms crept round his neck and they stood on the shore enjoying their first moments of physical contact. Carlos's arms tightened and his kisses became harder, more demanding. Gently Harriet broke away and looked at him pleadingly.

'No, Carlos. Don't rush me. Let's walk.'

He put his arm round her shoulders as they continued walking. She felt the contact of his body with a new awareness that thrilled and excited her. At the same time she knew she'd never felt safer or more secure with any one.

He continued their conversation: 'You've been badly hurt by someone.' It wasn't a question, but a statement.

'Yes,' she said slowly. Instinctively, as when they were talking on the terrace a few days before, she felt his sympathy and understanding. 'Shall we sit down?' They sat on the sand a few yards from the sea, his arms holding her close against him. Harriet began to talk. She told him everything about her marriage to Roger, his weakness and deception, his women, her need to cover up for the children's sake. Finally she told him of Roger's taunts of her lack of sexual attractiveness and her frigidity, things she'd not even told Emily.

He listened in silence, his arm tightening against her as she spoke of her husband's cruelty.

When she'd finished, the tears she'd kept so long inside, ran down her cheeks, slowly at first, then she was sobbing in his arms.

For a long time he held her against his chest, rubbing his face softly against her hair and stroking her with gentle hands.

At last she stopped crying and drawing slightly away from him dried her eyes and blew her nose fiercely on the handkerchief he'd taken from his pocket. With a sense of wonder she realised she felt freer and lighter of spirit than she'd been for years, exorcised at last of the ghost of Roger's hurts and petty taunts.

Looking up at Carlos, wanting to explain how she felt, she saw it was all unnecessary. Carlos knew, he'd been through it with her during the last few minutes, using the extraordinary gift of sensitivity that he possessed. He smiled and drew her back into his arms and gazed deep into her eyes. Suddenly his own dark eyes darkened even more and she lifted her lips to his. This time she was able to meet the passion in his kiss unafraid and felt he was drawing her soul into his. His kisses became urgent and demanding. Suddenly he pulled her to her feet and, picking her up as though she were a child, carried her towards an outcrop of rocks. Depositing her on the sand, he walked a few yards away and stood looking out to sea, his inner turmoil obvious from the tenseness of his body. She waited, her body on fire with her need of him, but saying nothing.

After a few minutes, he turned and dropped on his knees beside her.

'Harriet?' The word was a question, his voice harsh and almost unrecognisable. She held out her arms and with a groan he dropped on the sand, his arms around her, his mouth on her mouth, her cheeks, her neck until she was almost insensible with desire.

'Please, Carlos,' she whispered huskily and he took her in the moonlight, with the waves beating a gentle rhythm against the still-warm sand.

7

In all her years of marriage to Roger, even the earlier happier times, Harriet had not experienced such ecstacy. Carlos raised her to the heavens, slowly and tenderly at first, then when she was surely dying, sensations she'd not thought possible throbbed through her trembling body.

Hours later it seemed, she opened her eyes. He was lying on his side, head resting on one bent arm and gazing into her face with an expression, almost of wonder and she felt the ready tears once more slide down her face, this time tears of joy. He wiped then gently with his fingers then kissed her tenderly on her tingling lips.

'Oh, Carlos,' she breathed tremulously and his hands cupped her face as they lay side by side on the sand.

'I love you, Harriet,' he said. 'I've

loved you from that first moment when I watched you with my children. You were scolding the boys and trying to keep a straight face because you couldn't speak the language. You were wearing a bikini that left nothing to the imagination. Then I loved you even more when you tried to cover yourself up in front of me and I couldn't help teasing you by pretending not to notice you needed a wrap.'

Harriet laughed softly: 'I knew you were making fun of me, and it made me so cross.'

'You looked even more beautiful when you were angry. Oh, Harriet . . . ' His mouth traced a pattern over her cheek, brushed against her parted lips then swiftly met hers again in a passionate kiss. Afterwards they slept on the sand, clasped in each other's arms, their breath mingling in the warm night air and covered lightly by his jacket and her white shawl.

She was awakened by a sudden movement as Carlos sat up holding his left arm and with an expression of agony on his face. Fear clutched at her and she cried quickly: 'What's the matter? Are you ill, darling?'

'I've got cramp in my arm,' was the muttered reply. 'You were lying on it.' He grinned in spite of his obvious pain. 'You looked so peaceful I didn't want to disturb you.'

'You idiot,' she said softly, sitting up and taking his arm began to massage it.

'Madre de dios, you're hurting me!' he yelled, trying to draw his arm away. Relentlessly she continued, until the sheer ludicrousness of the situation hit her. She began to giggle, then dropped to the sand still clutching Carlos's arm as laughter overtook her. Carlos's look of astonishment turned to amusement and they lay on their backs laughing and giggling like two young children.

'We'd better get back to the car,' said Carlos at last, when their hilarity had subsided a little. 'It's getting quite cold.'

'I'm going to paddle in the sea first.'

Harriet got to her feet and ran towards the waves. Carlos picked up the jacket and shawl from the sand and following more sedately, watched her face as she dreamily danced in the shallows, stretching her toes sensuously in the cool, clear water.

'What are you thinking about?' he asked, seeming not to want even her thoughts to be a secret from him.

'Um . . . you,' she answered, smiling mysteriously at him.

He took her hands and gently pulled her from the sea edge, into his arms: 'What about me?'

'Oh . . . how I thought you were patronising and chauvinistic and I wasn't sure I even liked you.'

'And now?' He teased her lips with his mouth.

She drew her head away from his and regarded him seriously.

'I was fooling myself right from the start. I knew from that first meeting that I was falling in love with you. I couldn't get you out of my mind. And now . . . Carlos, we've known each other less than a week! It's not possible, but . . . I love you more than I ever dreamed I could love anyone, . . . ' her voice trembled and this time as they kissed, it was as though they were setting a seal on their love.

Later, as they sat in the car, reluctant to leave their own little paradise, Harriet asked mischievously:

'How did you know which was my bedroom window?'

'Perhaps I didn't,' he teased, 'perhaps I didn't mind which one of you women I woke up.'

She bit his finger which had been gently caressing her cheek and snuggled deeper against his broad shoulder.

Laughing, he said: 'You shouldn't lean out of your window in your nightdress at seven o'clock in the morning, exposing yourself to the neighbours. Shameless behaviour, but there, the English . . . ouch!' as she nipped his finger again with her beautiful white teeth.

'Anyway, you were out. Your car wasn't there.'

'So you were looking for me, were you?' He grinned at her. 'I was in my garden, fishing leaves from the pool and spying on your villa, hoping to catch a glimpse of you.'

'Were you?' she spoke wonderingly. 'But the car . . . ?'

'Consuela took the car to the market.' His fingers continued caressing her face.

Consuela . . . a dark cloud suddenly drifted across her mind. Hesitatingly — fearfully — she said, dreading his answer but knowing she had to ask:

'Carlos, who is Consuela?'

'She's my late wife's cousin. I thought I told you.'

'Yes, you did. But . . . what is her position in your house?'

Dropping his hand from her face, he turned his body and looked searchingly at her. A faint flush rose to her cheeks and she found she couldn't meet his eyes.

There was a long silence. She felt deathly cold.

At last he said slowly: 'She isn't my mistress, Harriet, if that's what you mean.' She opened her mouth to protest, but he went on quickly: 'But . . . I think she has, what is the English word? — aspirations. She came when my wife died, took over the running of the house, looked after the children and has been there ever since. It's like that in Spain. Families, however distant, help each other in times of need. Financially, she is quite independent. Her parents died several years ago in a cholera epidemic and left her some money and property. Because she was alone, she was the obvious one to come, but I think the family, both my side and that of my late wife and Consuela, expect us to marry eventually. Nothing has been said between Consuela and myself. I'm very fond of her and very grateful, but I don't love her and she doesn't love me.'

Harriet was silent. She believed

Carlos was wrong about Consuela's feelings toward himself. Then she said: 'She'll be very upset when she finds out about us. It seems rather cruel.' She felt a surge of sympathy for Consuela.

'Yes.' Carlos's voice was thoughtful. 'It will not be easy for her. I should have made the position clear before, but it didn't seem necessary. She always seemed quite happy the way things were and so was I. I'll have to tell her at once.'

'I don't think you need to, Carlos. She knows, I'm sure. I think she knew from the beginning, before I did.' Harriet felt she now knew the reason for Consuela's hostility. A woman in love is very perceptive about her man's feelings.

'You may be right — she has been behaving very strangely this week, hardly speaking to me and less patient with the children.'

'Actually,' said Harriet, 'I'd rather not say anything to anyone, yet.'

'Why not? You're not regretting . . . ?'

'Of course not,' she reached up and kissed him lovingly, 'but it's so sudden . . . '

He laughed boyishly: 'You mean they'll all think we're crazy. What does it matter.'

'Can't we keep it to ourselves a little while, enjoy our secret?' Harriet's voice was pleading.

'I want everyone to know I love you and am going to marry you as soon as possible.' He spoke firmly.

'Marry, but . . . ' suddenly Harriet felt afraid. She'd not thought of marriage, she'd not really thought of anything further than tonight.

'Of course, what did you think? That I only wanted you for this?' He indicated the beach, where they'd so recently made love. Taking her by the shoulders, he shook her gently. 'Harriet, I love you, don't you understand? I want to be with you always. This isn't just a passing affair — or is it for you?' His voice was suddenly harsh and his fingers bit into her shoulders. Harriet could hear the hurt in his voice. Quickly she said:

'No, of course it isn't, but . . . I'm only just divorced. To rush into another marriage straight away . . . ' Her voice faltered. All at once she felt desperately tired. He must have sensed this for he said gently: 'Come along darling. We'd better go home. We'll discuss it tomorrow.'

They spoke little on the short journey home and he pulled up in his driveway, quietly opening the doors. As they walked slowly towards her villa, arms entwined and bodies touching, Harriet shivered involuntarily. She'd touched the moon. Did she have the courage to grasp it in her hands?

Outside the villa Carlos kissed her tenderly. Harriet was reluctant to leave him, but he gently pushed her towards the house: 'Go and get some sleep, now. I'll see you in the morning.' Then he was gone into the darkness.

★　★　★

Harriet slept fitfully but was wide awake at seven o'clock. She lay in bed thinking of Carlos, her body heavy with longing for him. Pushing away all thoughts of the future, she tried to concentrate only on her love for the dark Spaniard who'd swept her off her feet.

She put on her dressing-gown and went downstairs. There was a letter on the mat. She picked it up and glanced at it without curiosity. A London postmark. It was from her solicitors — the formal notice of her decree absolute, granted a week ago. She'd forgotten all about it, since she'd informed her solicitors she would be in Spain. Her heart leaped — she was free of Roger at last!

Going into the kitchen still holding the letter, she switched on the electric coffee percolator and sat down at the table. Looking at the letter again, in a flash of insight she saw it for what it was. A piece of paper. A mere piece of paper saying her marriage was over. But her marriage was over years ago. She'd been wrong when she told Carlos her marriage was only just finished. She'd freed herself from Roger body and spirit a long time ago. The legality made no difference to how she felt.

She'd had years of loneliness, she didn't need time. All she needed was faith in herself and in Carlos and she knew she had that. A surge of happiness swept over her. She wanted to rush to Carlos and tell him how she felt, knowing how much she'd hurt him last night with her doubts. Smiling happily, she began to lay the breakfast table, determined to go to him straight after breakfast to tell him she wanted the whole world to know they were getting married!

'You look cheerful,' Ben's voice came from the doorway. He was dressed in dark trousers and a sports shirt, not his usual holiday attire.

'Are you going out?' Harriet asked in surprise. He took a mug from the hook and poured himself some coffee. 'I'm afraid I've got a bit of a shock for you, Mum.' Pulling out a chair, he sank into it wearily. 'I'm going home today.'

'But I thought you'd decided to go next week.' Harriet noted with dismay the wretched expression on her son's face.

'I was, but after the dinner last night Gabrielle and I had a long talk. Well, I've decided to go home — alone. That is, if you don't mind Gabrielle staying till the end of the week.' Harriet shook her head, her eyes fixed on Ben's face as he went on:

'We need to get some distance between us for a while. We've both got to think.'

'Gabrielle seemed very upset at your behaviour last night.'

'Yes, I did behave badly. I don't know what got into me.'

'It was rather unkind of you to involve Carlotta. She's an impressionable young girl.'

'I wasn't trying to make Gabrielle jealous, if that's what you think, Mum.

I was really knocked out by Carlotta. That's another reason why I think it's better for me to go home now. I think I could fall for her if I stayed and that would be really sick, wouldn't it?' Ben laughed bitterly. 'I'd like to go and say goodbye to her and try to put things right, but I don't really think it would be wise.'

'That's up to you, of course, Ben,' doubtfully, 'but perhaps you're right. She'll be a bit hurt, I expect, but I think she was also doing her share of the flirting. She must be used to having men pay her compliments, she's so attractive — anyway you don't want to make things more complicated than they already are. Things might seem clearer from a distance. Do you want any breakfast before you go?'

'No thanks, I'll stop on the road in an hour or so. Just another coffee, please. Then I'd better be off before the traffic starts piling up.'

Harriet didn't think the moment had come to break the news about

Carlos and herself.

Zoe appeared as Ben was finishing his coffee and was as surprised as her mother at his sudden departure. She was disappointed at losing a companion and when they'd waved Ben off and returned to the kitchen, she said: 'Why's Ben going without Gabrielle?'

'After last night I think they felt they needed some time apart to think things out.' Harriet put a cup of coffee in front of Zoe.

'What about last night?'

'Didn't you notice how well Ben and Carlotta were getting on? You'd have thought they were the engaged couple — not Ben and Gabrielle.'

Zoe shrugged. 'No, I can't say I noticed. Trust Gabrielle to get jealous, though. Anyway, I had a marvellous evening.' Her voice was dreamy.

'Ben and Gabrielle are going through a bad patch. It happens — especially during long engagements,' explained Harriet, trying to ignore the rapt expression on her daughter's face. 'Zoe?'

'Um . . . what?' Zoe was absently munching a piece of cold toast. 'Sorry — what did you say?'

'I thought you wanted to know about Ben and Gabrielle,' answered her mother in some amusement, 'but obviously your mind is elsewhere.'

Zoe was silent and Harriet began to clear away the dirty dishes. It was getting late and she must shower and change if she was going to see Carlos.

As she hastily washed up, Zoe came behind her and picking up a tea-towel, said:

'Mummy, I'm in love with Carlos and I think he feels the same way about me.' Her voice was serious and unchildlike.

Harriet's heart stopped beating momentarily, then thudded into action, making her feel suddenly dizzy.

'You're joking,' she tried to laugh, but no sound came from her dry lips.

'I've never been so serious in my life. Oh, Mummy, I feel wonderful. I knew the first time I met him, but last night I could tell he felt the same. Didn't you notice how he singled me out, how we laughed and talked so much together. The look in his eyes made me feel weak all over and when we said goodbye he said he'd be seeing me again — very soon.' Her voice was clear and confident.

Harriet was silent. Carlos *had* appeared to pay especial attention to Zoe. It was one of the many incidents that had been depressing the night before. Not that she thought Carlos was attracted to her daughter in that way. She knew, after last night that Carlos was hers alone. But during the dinner, she had felt just the faintest tinge of jealousy, more of Zoe's youth than of her daughter herself. 'Oh, Carlos,' thought Harriet in anguish, 'what have you done? And what do I do now, what do I say?'

8

After she'd showered and dressed and struggled to think rationally about the latest predicament, Harriet went into the garden to cut some flowers for the living-room. It was something to do while she waited for Carlos. He'd said last night he'd see her in the morning, but not mentioned a time.

The front door opened and Zoe emerged wearing her one and only cotton dress and high-heeled sandals instead of the usual jeans and jumper. She waved blithely to her mother. 'I'm just going to see Carlotta,' she called. 'Don't expect me back for lunch.'

Harriet waved acknowledgment, thinking sombrely 'Carlotta or Carlos?' She wondered once again at Zoe's quick changes of mood, so like her father's. Perhaps this schoolgirl crush for Carlos would vanish as quickly as it had arisen.

Harriet knew that Carlos would not wait for such an event, supposing it did happen, before announcing their own plans for marriage. He was coming this morning for Harriet's yes or no, and she knew he wouldn't accept any indecision on her part.

As she arranged the beautiful, highly-scented mimosa in a porcelain vase, Harriet felt her heart would break, knowing what she had to do now was the hardest thing she'd ever done in her life. Was it only two hours ago she'd been so sure her answer would be yes? It seemed a lifetime away.

He came in quickly through the open french doors; taking her in his arms tenderly and possessively. As she responded instinctively to his kiss she knew she was trembling from head to foot, part in passion, part in despair.

'Carlos, not here,' she murmured unsteadily, pulling herself from his arms. 'Gabrielle might come in.'

Laughing lightly, and not releasing her hands, he drew her to the settee. 'I don't care who comes in, my darling. Let the whole world see us.' He reached for her again, his kiss brushing her cheek as she quickly turned her face away.

His laughter died. Gently turning her face towards him he saw the tears rolling steadily down her cheeks. 'What's the matter? What's happened?'

She couldn't speak, the silent tears and misery in her eyes bringing an anxious frown to his handsome face.

'I came this morning for your answer and I thought you gave it to me in your kiss. Was I mistaken, Harriet? Don't tell me you're going to reject me?' The pleading note in the voice of this strong, forceful man was almost too much for Harriet to bear. Her resolution weakened for seconds, then, drawing a deep breath, she said brokenly,

'Have you seen Zoe?'

'Zoe?' he was puzzled. 'Yes, she called to see Carlotta just as I was leaving. Why?'

'Did you speak to her?' Harriet persisted.

'Briefly, but I was in a hurry. She looked alright. In fact she was positively radiant. I remarked on it.'

'You would,' said Harriet bitterly.

He seemed surprised at her tone. 'What is it, Harriet? What has Zoe got to do with all this?'

'Only that she's in love with you, or thinks she is, and is convinced that you love her too.' She met his eyes, shocked to find she was suddenly angry with him.

His look was incredulous. 'Zoe . . . and me? But what has given her that idea? I've never . . . ' he stopped, realisation dawning on his face.

'Yes,' she answered steadily, 'last night at dinner your attentions were very noticeable. Even to me. It made me . . . wonder.'

'Madre de dios,' he swore softly under his breath. 'I didn't expect her to . . . I didn't mean . . . All I was doing, my darling Harriet, was to try to charm the daughter of the woman I love. To get her on my side, you would say in England. I didn't dream she'd think . . . I'm old enough to be her father!'

'You underestimate the strength of your attractiveness, Carlos,' Harriet said dryly, her heart nevertheless lifting at the undoubted truth of his explanation.

'The poor girl, how thoughtless of me. I should have known better with a young daughter of my own. We'll have to explain right away,' he said firmly, taking her hands in his once again.

'It's not as simple as that. I don't think you realize the seriousness of the situation. She thinks she's in love with you, really in love. How can we be so cruel as to tell her just now that it's me, her mother, you love?'

'But we have to — it's the only way. She's got to know sometime and because of this, the sooner the better.'

'I don't agree. I think we should wait. Perhaps she'll get over it soon, she has these crushes quite often, though usually with boys of her own age. Then we can break the news to her.'

'How soon is 'soon' likely to be, Harriet? Two days, two weeks, two years?'

'There's no way of knowing, but hopefully when we get back to England . . . '

'But that's four weeks away . . . You can't be serious! And what do *we* do in the meantime? Shake hands politely over the cups of tea?' His words were sarcastic, obviously covering up for the hurt he was feeling.

'Can't we continue meeting in secret for a while?' she said hesitantly.

'No, Harriet. I told you last night, I do not want an affair with you. I want to marry you with all the family on both sides watching. What happened last night . . . . it mustn't happen again until we're legally man and wife. And, darling, I cannot wait for that day. It must be as soon as we can possibly arrange it.' His hands tightened on hers convulsively and her heart thudded in response to the passion in his eyes.

She must be strong! 'Carlos, I can't. I can't hurt Zoe again. It hurt her very deeply when she thought I'd sent Roger away. She hated me for it and misses him terribly. Now she'll feel I'm deliberately taking you away from her. We know that isn't the case, but in the mood she's in she'll not listen to the facts. Can't you understand, Carlos. You're making me choose between you and Zoe. Whatever I do I'll hurt one of you. But she's so young. And she'll never forgive me. All I'm asking is that we wait until we get back to England and then perhaps you could come to London . . . ' Her voice trailed off as he dropped her hands and stood up abruptly, walking across the room to the doors which were open on to the terrace. He stood there staring across the garden.

'Carlos?' she faltered watching his cold, forbidding expression.

'No, Harriet. I think there's more behind all this than Zoe's supposed feelings for me. You are afraid to commit yourself again and are using this as an excuse.'

Harriet gasped with shock at his words: 'No, Carlos!'

He continued as if she'd not spoken. 'You must decide now. Either we tell Zoe and everyone else immediately and arrange the wedding, or we'll never see each other again.' He turned to see the effect of his ultimatum. She was white to the lips and staring at him wordlessly. 'Well?' He spoke gently. 'I cannot wait for you indefinitely, Harriet. Who knows how long this will go on? You must choose now.'

Tearing her eyes from his implacable face, she looked down at her hands. Once more the tears began to fall and she watched them sliding between her tightly clasped fingers.

Carlos moved quickly from the window and, sitting beside her again, he turned her face towards his. Quickly, intensely, he said: 'Harriet, be sensible. We can't let a schoolgirl crush ruin our lives. What you and I have is something special, something real — or I thought it was. Is it — or am I wrong?'

Harriet nodded, raising her tear-filled eyes to his. 'You know it is, Carlos. But Zoe, I can't hurt her again. Her feeling for you is just as real to her as mine is to me. She's so young, so vulnerable.'

'But it's because she's so young that she'll get over it quickly. We must tell her now. It will be hurtful, I know, but she will recover. She'll find someone nearer her own age in no time and it will be as though I didn't exist. You know that more than I do, you've had more experience with young people. But you and I, Harriet, are different. The feeling we have between us comes once in a lifetime and we can't afford to throw it away. We're neither of us getting any younger . . .'

He tried to inject a lightness in to his tone. Harriet responded with a wry smile wiping the tears with the back of her hand.

'I know you're right, Carlos, but it doesn't alter the fact that it's me, her own mother, doing the hurting, for the second time in her short life.' Harriet's eyes were sombre. 'Please, Carlos, can't we wait a few weeks. I'll go back to England now, take Zoe with me, make some excuse . . . '

'No, Harriet. It must be done now. Before she has time to build up more impossible hopes.' He pulled her resisting body towards him, placing his warm, demanding mouth to her cold, unresponsive lips. Try as she could, Harriet could not resist the feeling that swept over her at his touch. Her treacherous body, so easily controlled over the past few years, burst the tight restraint she'd kept on it since Carlos came into the room and desire such as she'd never experienced before pervaded her whole being as she returned his kiss.

They drew apart, both shaken by the depth of their feeling for each other. Carlos's eyes burned into Harriet's. She knew, despite her very strong resolution of that morning, she could never let

Carlos go. He was right. Zoe would recover, would forgive her in time. 'Oh, please God, let her forgive me,' she prayed silently.

'We'll tell Zoe,' she said softly and he grasped her hands tightly as if willing her not to change her mind.

'When will she be back?'

'She said not for lunch, so I don't expect her until this evening, for dinner.'

'We'll tell her then. But now, my love, I want you all to myself. It's pointless waiting here, you'll only worry. I know a little place in the mountains, not far away where we can have lunch. We'll talk about our future — our future together.' His voice was caressing, his eyes glowing and now she'd made her decision she caught the infection of his mood.

'I'll leave a note for Gabrielle, she's gone for a walk. Won't be a minute.' Gaily she kissed him on the lips, and, roguishly evading his reaching arms, darted from the room.

★ ★ ★

They held hands on the journey to the mountains, Carlos only releasing her in order to change gear. Fortunately there was little traffic on the road, a mere track winding gently upwards.

Talking all the time, wanting to know everything about each other from as early as their memories could take them, they marvelled at the difference in their up-bringing. Carlos had been brought up in a very strict household, among several brothers and sisters, and had been taught the family business from an early age. Harriet, on the other hand, had spent her early life the only child of elderly, doting parents, who spared no expense on her education and welfare. Roger had been jealous of her deep, protective love for her gentle mother and absent-minded intellectual father, resenting her frequent visits to them until their tragic deaths, within months of each other a few years ago.

Harriet discovered with amazed

delight that Carlos had stayed only a few streets from Harriet's own home in London when he'd come to England as part of his business training. 'But I was married then and you were only a boy,' she said half-laughingly, bringing into the open another of the concerns about their whirlwind relationship.

'I wasn't a boy — I was eighteen when I came to England,' he shrugged unconcernedly.

'I already had Ben then. Quite the young matron I was, pushing my pram round the park, showing off my baby.'

They'd parked the car and were strolling along a deserted mountain track which offered superb views of the surrounding countryside.

'If I'd seen you then I'd have fallen in love with you, baby or no baby. I'd have kidnapped you and taken you off to Spain.'

'Don't you mind that I'm older than you?' she said in between bursts of laughter. This was a new Carlos, boyish

and light-hearted. Gone was the sophisticated charmer as he'd been at the
dinner in his villa, with his practised
flattery and teasing glances.

'I always preferred mature women,'
his voice was lecherous, his eyes
narrowed as he pretended to drag her
into the undergrowth. At the look of
consternation on her face, he pulled her
into his arms and kissed her soundly.

'Oh, Carlos. I've never been so happy
as I am at this moment,' she said when
she got back her breath. She snuggled
into his shoulder as they walked again
along the tree-lined path.

Suddenly his voice was serious. 'Is
there anything else worrying you,
Harriet? Your daughter, our ages,
Consuela, our different countries, my
children.' He counted on his fingers as
he listed the various problems she was
anticipating.

'You forgot to mention my son and
his fiancée, or ex-fiancée, I don't know
what she is at the moment, my job, your
family and I don't mean your children.'

'We'll think about all those things when the time comes and not before. Certainly not now, my darling. Kiss me again,' he demanded.

As they stood, arms around each other, it seemed they were alone in the world, everyone ceased to exist for Harriet but Carlos.

Later they lunched at a delightful small cantina nestling in the trees by the side of the mountain pass. As she devoured mouthfuls of the deliciously light omelette Harriet realised how hungry she was. She'd barely eaten for twenty-four hours — practically nothing at the dinner. Was that only yesterday? she thought in silent amazement? So much had happened in that short space of time.

'A penny for your thoughts?' Carlos' voice was amused. She met his eyes above the rim of the glass as she sipped the delicately flavoured wine he had carefully chosen for the occasion.

Seriously she said: 'Is this me, Carlos? Sitting here with you, a man I met only a week ago? I feel I've known you forever. You know I can't believe how uncharacteristically I've behaved. I don't rush into things, I usually think carefully and weigh up the pros and cons. I'm quite shy with people, especially men, but with you . . . ' She stopped, unable to express the amazement she felt.

'Don't question it, darling, just accept it for what it is. Fate.' For a moment Carlos looked anxious. 'Do you regret it, Harriet? Last night, I mean?'

She looked at him steadily, putting down her glass and reaching both hands to clasp his. 'No! It was the most wonderful experience of my life. I wanted you desperately. It was probably the most honest thing I've ever done.' Her voice trembled and at her words, his hands tightened on hers. Desire for him flooded through her body. His voice thickened as they stared into each other's eyes. 'Harriet, I love you. I want you now.'

He got up abruptly and throwing some money on the table, pulled her to her feet. They went to the car, Harriet's legs following where he led. Barely waiting for her to close the door behind her, he started the engine violently and drove onto the road with screech of over-acceleration. She clutched his arm as they narrowly avoided an on-coming car, but Carlos appeared not to notice.

He drove swiftly along the narrow road, turning between a small avenue of trees and drove deep into the small forest. Stopping the car he got out and went to the boot from which he took a large plaid travelling rug. Feeling she was in a dream, Harriet took the rug from him and spread it on the grass of the small clearing in the trees where Carlos had brought her.

He took her roughly, without tenderness and Harriet cried aloud at her fulfilment.

Breathing heavily, he held her tightly in his arms and to her amazement she felt his tears on her face.

'Forgive me, darling,' he half-groaned. 'You make me crazy. I don't know what got into me. Please forgive me.'

Harriet didn't reply, her face turned away from him. Desperately, he pulled her face towards him and looked into her eyes. What he saw there made his eyes widen in astonishment.

She was radiant, her eyes heavy with passion fulfilled, her face glowing with adoration for him. Unbelievingly he sat up and looked at her lovely slumbrous face. Slowly he smiled: 'Madre de dios, what kind of woman have I got? You enjoyed it, Harriet Maxwell. Have you no shame?'

She reached up, putting her arms round his neck and pulled him down beside her: 'No shame at all, Carlos Mendoza. I should have warned you. We have a saying in England. Something about not waking a sleeping tiger. I think you've done just that, my love.'

This time their love-making was slow, tender and deeply emotional. Harriet felt that nothing could ever come between them, so closely bound were they now, emotionally and physically.

They drove home in deep contentment, hands linked, bodies touching, not bearing to be apart.

He stopped the car outside her villa, promising to come in one hour's time at six o'clock so they could talk to Zoe together. He called her back to the car twice to kiss her again and Harriet was so happy she didn't care who saw them.

9

At ten to six Harriet went to the window and saw Carlos coming from his villa and from the opposite direction, from the town, Zoe was approaching. The met at the villa gate and the joy in Zoe's face was apparent, although Carlos wore a noticeably casual, but friendly, expression on his face as he greeted her.

They entered together, Carlos' eyes fixing themselves reassuringly on Harriet's anxious face.

'Look who I met outside, Mother,' said Zoe gaily, indicating their visitor. 'Carlos said you've got something to tell me. What is it?' She settled herself on the arm of a chair and looked at them both enquiringly.

'Won't you sit down, Carlos?' asked Harriet, her voice sounding formal as though she were greeting a mere acquaintance. Carlos obeyed, raising an ironic eyebrow.

'What is it, Mum?' repeated Zoe, dismissing the formalities with youthful impatience.

There was a small silence, then Carlos, getting up from his chair went to sit next to Harriet on the settee, taking her cold hand in his.

Zoe's eyes widened and a look of incredulity and shock appeared, wiping the gay smile from her face.

'Carlos and I,' began Harriet, taking a deep breath, 'we are . . . '

At that moment they heard the sound of a car stopping outside, slamming doors and running footsteps towards the villa. Zoe, dragging her eyes from the clasped hands of her mother and the Spaniard, ran to the window.

'It's daddy!' She raced to open the front door as Harriet and Carlos rose, looking at each other in amazement. Harriet felt herself go icy cold. What was Roger doing here? And at this particularly inopportune moment.

They turned as Roger entered, followed closely by Zoe who had a strange look, almost of triumph, thought the stunned Harriet.

'Harriet, darling!' Roger's voice brought Harriet's eyes to face her former husband and the next moment she was enveloped in a bearlike hug, and Roger kissed her passionately on the mouth before she could resist. Tearing herself away from him, she demanded furiously: 'What are you doing here?'

He smiled at her, seemingly unperturbed at the lack of welcome in her manner: 'I got your telegram this morning. I took the first available flight.'

'What telegram?' asked Harriet faintly as she heard an exclamation and felt a slight withdrawal from Carlos, who'd been standing at her side regarding the three Maxwells in some confusion.

Roger reached into his inside pocket and drew out a folded paper, which Harriet almost snatched from him.

She read: 'ROGER. PLEASE COME DARLING I NEED YOU. EVER YOURS HARRIET.'

Unbelievingly she looked at Roger, then her eyes turned towards Carlos who took the telegram from her unresisting hand. His eyes scanned the words and she saw his face harden.

'What's the meaning of this?' He directed his words at Harriet, ignoring the other two occupants of the room. She shook her head wordlessly, unable to speak. His lips tightened and thrusting the telegram into her hands, he turned on his heel and strode furiously from the room.

The suddenness of his action startled Harriet's numbed mind into action and pushing past Roger and Zoe crying 'Carlos!' she ran quickly after the departing Spaniard. He didn't turn. 'Carlos!' she called again. 'I didn't send that telegram.' By this time he was half-way up the hill towards his villa and Harriet's words floated in the empty space between them.

Harriet stared after his retreating back in horror and disbelief then, feeling she was in the middle of a nightmare but knowing this was even more terrible, she turned slowly and walked towards the door, heedless of the tears running down her face.

'Who was that fellow?' Roger's blustering voice trailed off as he saw Harriet's face.

She stood inside the door, leaning against the jambe as if for support. Tiredly she looked at Roger and Zoe in turn then, her face hardening but not bothering to wipe away the tears: 'I didn't send the telegram, so who did?' Her eyes rested on Zoe's suddenly pale face. The girl looked desperately towards her father, but he was watching Harriet, realisation dawning on his handsome, dissolute face.

'Did you send the telegram, Zoe?' Harriet's voice was quiet and controlled, the despair she felt inside tightly reigned.

Zoe was silent, her eyes entreating

her father to support her, as he so often had when she'd misbehaved as a child, but the face he slowly turned to her was cold and condemning. 'Did you?' he asked, as if speaking to a stranger.

She sank on to the settee and buried her head in her hands. 'I was doing it for you,' she sobbed. 'I knew you wanted Mummy back, and this seemed a good opportunity. I'd been thinking about it for a long time, and when Ben said he thought Carlos . . . Senor Mendoza . . . was . . . interested in Mother . . and she . . . was falling for him . . . I thought I'd better send for you . . . before it was too late. I . . . thought you'd be . . . sure to come . . . if you thought . . . it was . . . Mother . . . sending . . . for you.' Harriet watched her daughter's tears but felt no pity. She had no feelings left inside her.

★ ★ ★

How long she lay on her bed staring at the ceiling she could not tell. Repeated knocking at the door finally roused her from a state of semi-consciousness.

Gabrielle came into the room carrying a tray. 'Are you alright?' she asked. 'I've brought you some food. Harriet, I overheard, I'm so sorry.'

Suddenly Harriet felt the ice which seemed to cover her mind begin to crack. She shuddered convulsively and all the emotions she'd tried to keep out, crowded in on her. With a moan of utter despair, she began to cry, racking sobs seeming to tear apart her whole body.

'Oh, Harriet.' Gabrielle gathered her in her arms, as if she was the older of the two and rocked the grief-stricken woman like a baby.

When at last the spasm passed, Harriet looked at Gabrielle through red-rimmed eyes, with a faint glimmer of her usual spirit.

'What do I do now? Carlos will never forgive me. Perhaps if I go to him I can make him listen. Yes, that's what I'll do.' She began to get off the bed, running her fingers through her tousled hair.

'Harriet,' Gabrielle spoke gently. 'He's gone.'

'Gone? Gone where?'

'I don't know, but I was looking from my bedroom window an hour ago. He put a couple of suitcases in the car and drove off. The whole family was there to wave goodbye.'

Harriet stared at the other woman in horror. Finding her legs could no longer support her, she dropped on to the bed: 'And I was lying here feeling sorry for myself. I should have gone after him straight away,' she murmured dully. The despair was back in her voice and she suddenly felt very old.

Her mind a blank, she sat motionless for a few minutes, then pulling herself together visibly got up and walked to the dressing-table. 'Well, that's that. Thanks Gabrielle. I'll be alright. I'll just tidy myself up and come downstairs. It's no good staying up here brooding, that won't bring him back.' Harriet's voice broke momentarily, then taking a deep breath, she continued: 'Where's Roger? And Zoe?'

'They're both in the living-room. Roger's made himself at home. He's drinking your whisky — he's had half a bottle already.' Gabrielle's voice was dry. There was obviously no deep affection between her and Ben's father.

'That figures,' Harriet replied in the same tone, stepping out of her creased and crumpled dress, and walking towards the bathroom.

Roger greeted her with his charming smile. His face was flushed as he said, his words slurring a little: 'Feeling better, old lady?'

His choice of words could be more tactful, thought Harriet wryly. She felt like an old lady. Without answering directly she said: 'We have to talk, Roger — and Zoe.'

Zoe was sitting in the corner of the settee, her eyes red, pretending to read a book. There was the familiar sulky droop to her mouth.

'I'll have one of those, please, Roger.'

Harriet indicated the whisky glass by Roger's side.

'Oh . . . yes, of course.' He was unembarrassed and picked up his own glass for a refill. 'I helped myself. I hope you don't mind.'

Handing her the drink, he went on in an aggrieved voice: 'I want to know what's going on here. I arrived expecting a reconcilation with my wife and find a strange dago holding her hand, not even acknowledging my existence.'

Harriet felt her nerve-ends tingle. 'Ex-wife,' she interposed coldly. 'And Senor Mendoza is not a dago.'

'Mendoza, eh? So that's his name, is it? Who is he anyway and what's he to you?'

Harriet looked at Roger, seeing his eyes glazed with drink, his self-righteous manner, then at Zoe, who had given up her pretence of reading and was regarding her parents resentfully. Suddenly Harriet wanted to shock these two people who were bent on destroying her happiness.

'Carlos Mendoza is my lover and we are — were — going to be married.'

The silence that followed her flat statement was shattering. Roger's face became even more suffused and Zoe looked stricken.

'Oh, my God,' thought Harriet, 'I've gone too far.' She leaned across and stretched out a pleading hand to her daughter, who seemed dazed, unable to take in what she had heard.

'I'm sorry, Zoe. I didn't mean you to find out like this. Carlos and I wanted to break it to you gently — that's what we wanted to discuss with you this evening, when your father so inopportunely arrived.'

Zoe brushed aside the outstretched hand and glared at her mother: 'You did it on purpose — because you knew he liked me. You deliberately went after him. I saw you at the dinner trying to make up to him, but he preferred to talk to me, it was obvious. I bet you seduced him. A woman of your age — it's disgusting!'

Zoe's voice was shrill with spite and Harriet felt her daughter's suffering equal to her own. 'That's not true Zoe, anyhow he's gone now and you've achieved your object. I don't suppose I shall ever see him again.'

10

The doctor's voice rang in her ears. 'I'm afraid he'll have to stay in bed. He certainly cannot travel until he has recovered.'

Furiously Harriet glared at Roger, who was lying in bed, his face yellow-tinged, eyes bloodshot. 'He'll have to go to hospital,' she said shortly, 'there's no-one to look after him here.'

'That's impossible, Mrs. Maxwell,' answered the English-speaking Spanish doctor politely, 'our hospitals are over-worked at present and we can only take in emergencies. While Mr. Maxwell is very sick, it is not serious. All he needs is rest, good nourishing food and absolutely no alcohol.' He emphasised the last three words and Roger closed his eyes against the note of censure in the doctor's voice.

'I can't have him here, doctor,'

Harriet insisted as she followed the doctor downstairs. 'He's not my husband, we're divorced.'

'I'm sorry. It is awkward for you, but there's nothing I can do.' The doctor was sympathetic. Harriet looked truly distraught. 'You could send him to a private clinic. I'm afraid the cost is rather high.'

'How high?' demanded Harriet desperately. Anything but to have Roger in the house.

The doctor mentioned a sum which made Harriet's eyes widen in dismay. 'How long will he be ill?' she asked.

'Who can say?' the doctor shrugged. 'It depends how long he's been drinking heavily. If it's only recent, then perhaps one or two weeks, but if it's been going on a long time, it could be months.'

Harriet was horrified. She knew she couldn't afford the sum mentioned by the doctor. It was unlikely that Roger had taken out medical insurance before he left England, coming at such short notice, and she doubted, that he could afford a private clinic's fee.

The doctor stood diffidently by the front door, and as Harriet saw him out she thanked him for his help, thinking how fortunate it was she'd been able to find a doctor who could speak English. She'd never have been able to understand the technical jargon in Spanish!

Going back upstairs, her mind was on the present predicament she found herself in. Having Roger in the house was more than she could bear after the events of yesterday. How long had he been drinking heavily? She knew he had always enjoyed a drink as he liked to put it, and seemed to go to the whisky bottle rather frequently in the latter years of their marriage, but he prided himself on never actually getting drunk, whatever that meant! She'd often remarked upon his drinking only to be accused of nagging and her comments only gave him the excuse to assert his independence by drinking more.

Now he was in danger of damaging

his liver permanently if he did not stop.

'How long has this been going on?' she demanded as she entered the small bedroom, where Ben had slept during his visit.

Roger didn't answer, keeping his eyes closed.

'You'll have to co-operate if you're going to stay here. Otherwise you must go somewhere else. The doctor told me just now there are places . . . ' she went on, hardening herself against her natural sympathy. Roger did look poorly, but it was his own fault, she told herself sternly.

'What sort of places?' he asked fearfully. A glimmer of pity seeped through her shell of resistance.

'Private clinics.'

'You mean for alcoholics? I'm not an alcoholic, Harriet. I admit I've been hitting the bottle quite hard recently, especially since we broke up . . . ' His voice took on a self-pitying tone.

'Why, oh why, does he always have the power to make me feel the guilty one?' thought Harriet resentfully. 'I'll get you some breakfast,' she said out loud, but he caught her hand as she turned away.

'Harriet, I'm sorry.' His voice was sincere, and she looked at him in surprise. 'I didn't mean to cause you all this trouble. I did intend to go this morning, but I don't think I've ever felt so ill. Please let me stay. I'll try not to be a nuisance and cause you more trouble.

The appeal in his voice drove away her resentment and hostility, but she withdrew her hand from his and continued towards the door.

'Harriet?' Roger's voice was almost conspiratorial. 'Was it true about you and Mendoza being lovers?'

She stood still without turning. 'Yes, it was,' she replied in a low voice.

'It's alright, I don't blame you. In fact, it puts us on the same level now, doesn't it? My women friends and your Spaniard. Now he's gone, can't we start again — on equal terms?' He laughed.

Stifling the scream that rose to her lips, she felt the blood pound in her head. Slowly she turned towards Roger and looking him fully in his smugly-smiling face, said slowly and distinctly:

'Don't ever put Carlos Mendoza in the same category as 'your women'. You and I will never be equal in that or in anything else. I will look after you until you are able to travel, but remember this. I despise you, Roger, and I'll *never* go back to you. In fact, once you're on the plane to England, I don't ever want to see you again. Not ever.'

Breathing deeply she went downstairs, fighting against the sickness that rose in her stomach, leaving an astonished and highly offended Roger speechless for the first time in his life.

★   ★   ★

Later that morning, Zoe, whom Harriet hadn't seen since the night before, arrived with Carlotta and the three young Mendoza children. Harriet greeted the Mendozas warmly, with a quick glance at the unresponsive face of her daughter.

'We're going to the beach,' announced Zoe, obviously anxious to be away. 'Consuela's gone shopping and left the children with Carlotta. I've come for my swimming things.' Her voice was cold and formal and she addressed the kitchen table rather than look directly at her mother, whilst giving a brief explanation of their plans. While she was upstairs, Harriet sent the children, biscuits in every available hand, into the garden and tried to make conversation with a noticeably uncommunicative Carlotta.

'I understand your father has gone away.' Harriet's voice was casual.

'Si,' answered the Spanish girl briefly, sipping the coffee Harriet had poured for her.

'Is he gone for long?' pursued Harriet.

'I don't know,' was the reply, accompanied by an indifferent shrug.

With determination, Harriet persevered. 'Where has he gone? Did he leave an address? He asked me to lend him some English magazines, perhaps I could send them on to him if he's not coming home soon . . . ' she improvised hesitantly.

Carlotta put down her coffee cup. 'He left his address with Consuela. She is the only person who knows where he will be. Consuela sends our letters when he is away. That is natural as she will be our mother one day. If you'd like to give me the . . . magazines . . . I'll ask Consuela to forward them for you if you wish.' Her voice was deliberate and she looked into Harriet's eyes, her own hard and cool. Harriet recoiled in shock at the hostility there, then, forcing a polite smile she replied: 'I wouldn't like to put Consuela to that trouble. It doesn't matter. It's not important.'

At that moment, Zoe returned to the kitchen, beach bag in her hand. Carlotta joined her in the doorway and the two girls stood, arms linked, regarding the stricken Harriet.

'So that's the way it is,' thought Harriet wryly. 'They're allies now, and I must be the enemy.' Carlotta said tersely: 'The children don't want to come to the beach with us, they want to stay here.'

Zoe glanced at her mother indifferently. 'Can they?'

Harriet looked at the pleading expression in the children's eyes. 'Of course they can, as long as you're back by lunch-time. They'll probably be bored by then.' She felt the girls would be little company for the children at this particular time and watched them depart, arms intertwined, obviously relieved at the shedding of their three little burdens.

Harriet regarded the now silent children, suddenly aware of the language barrier that existed now Carlotta was gone. She searched her mind and was able to indicate in short phrases of her imperfect Spanish that they should play in the garden, but must not climb the trees. She didn't want to have to cope with any accidents if at all possible. The children giggled in delight at the English woman's Spanish and she grinned back: 'You must help me speak Spanish,' she ventured further and they all nodded, hands over their mouths to stifle their amusement.

As Harriet busied herself with the few chores that must be done in spite of the children's presence, she realized with pleasure that at last she was going to have an opportunity to get to know them. A little late, she felt sadly, but since their meeting at the pool, she'd had little contact with the youngest Mendozas, they were in bed during the dinner at their villa, and Consuela made sure they stayed in their own garden during the day.

Harriet loved children and, more importantly, felt that any link with Carlos was better than the despairing emptiness without him.

Gabrielle returned from the market almost immediately. She'd offered to do the shopping whilst Harriet received the doctor. Harriet was grateful for the girl's quiet support. She felt Gabrielle was the only friend and ally she had in Spain and the two women had become very close.

When Gabrielle heard what the doctor had told Harriet, she said sympathetically: 'Poor Harriet, As if you've not got enough to cope with.'

'What about you?' demanded Harriet with a wry smile. 'This hasn't exactly been a dream holiday for you. How are you coping without Ben?'

Gabrielle's face clouded for a moment. 'I miss him terribly, of course, but I know it was essential to get some distance between us. I confused him terribly when I changed my 'image'. I should have discussed it with him first, but I knew if I didn't do it at once I might not have the courage later. I gambled on his love for me, I only pray I haven't lost him.'

After that day Carlotta regularly left her little brothers and sister with

Harriet whilst she went to the beach with Zoe and her friends.

The children were becoming very attached to Harriet, whom they called Senora Harriet, and even the boys didn't resist an affectionate kiss, lightly given. Maria was less inhibited and often crept on to Harriet's lap, a picture book or pencil and paper in her hand and Harriet taught her to knit with wool and needles brought from the market. She taught them all English nursery rhymes and they, in turn, sang their own little songs to her. She realized with a pang how much the children missed a mother's love, Consuela being too busy to spend much time with them, Carlotta often away at school.

She found, without surprise, the boys respected her firmness with them. They knew, however much fun and mischief she allowed them, just how far to go. Often she wondered what Consuela thought of the children's visits to her, but one day as Carlotta was leaving with the children, Harriet overheard her mentioning Consuela's name with a warning note in her voice.

She tackled Carlotta the next day, asking if Consuela knew of the children's visits. The girl shrugged indifferently and replied she hadn't thought it necessary, but that Consuela would stop the visits if she knew. The thought of not having the children's company made Harriet ignore her own misgivings at the deception for the time being.

Her real fears were for when she left Spain. Would the children feel abandoned, as they must have done when their mother died? She knew she would feel the loss very deeply herself, but she existed without Carlos every day and nothing could be worse than that. She was desperate to explain to him, but feared now she would never have the opportunity to do so.

11

Harriet was surprised at the change in Roger since his illness. He'd stopped complaining after the first week or so, mainly she suspected because of Gabrielle's firm and matter-of-fact attitude towards him. Gabrielle had long since taken over the bulk of Roger's nursing, obviously noticing how tired and strained Harriet was becoming through his constant demands on her time and attention. Harriet now visited his room only when it was absolutely necessary, seeing to those personal tasks such as bathing him or changing his linen, jobs she could hardly hand over to the younger woman.

But now as they sat by the pool, Roger quietly reading and frequently sipping his orange juice, Harriet saw the lines of dissipation had softened, the reddish tinge to his skin had

165

disappeared, leaving his face pale. She noticed the grey specks in his blonde hair and the once clear eyes shadowed and tired. Unexpectedly, a wave of sympathy for him surged over her.

'Is this what I've done to you, Roger,' she thought. 'And will I be the same as you in a few years' time, without Carlos?' She closed her eyes against the pain which suddenly invaded her heart.

'What's the matter, Harriet?' A light touch on her arm accompanying the softly spoken words startled her and she met Roger's eyes, her own brimming with tears, frankly and undefenceless for the first time since he'd arrived.

They were alone. The children had gone for once to the beach with the girls and Gabrielle had borrowed Harriet's car to go to Malaga for the day.

'Are you very unhappy?' went on Roger in the same sympathetic tone.

She nodded, unable to speak.

'Is there anything I can do? I seem to be the cause of your unhappiness. And not just recently. You know, Harriet, I've had a lot of time to think lately, lying in bed, my head clear of the booze for a change.' He managed a rueful grin. 'I've been a real swine to you, haven't I?'

She nodded again, slowly, and his grin changed to a grimace.

'I'd like to make it up to you. It's not very pleasant, seeing yourself clearly for the first time. I used to think I was a great chap, and that you didn't appreciate me. Everyone else liked me, even loved me, but you always seemed to look down on me. I couldn't understand it. But of course, I know now. You knew me, the real me, others only saw what I wanted them to see.' He sighed, then continued: 'But I can change. I nearly did before — even Ben noticed. After I went away.'

Harriet remembered Ben telling her so when he arrived at the villa.

Roger was still talking in a low, unemotional voice, so unlike his usual boisterous bluster. 'I cut down the drink, I hadn't had a woman for months.' Harriet winced, but he appeared not to notice, carrying on steadily: 'Then suddenly, one day I realised you weren't ever going to take me back. That was the day I came to the house to invite you to dinner. I brought you some flowers. Remember?'

Harriet remembered. 'Yes Roger. They were more expensive than I had ever had.'

'I can imagine what you thought,' he said quietly. 'I was damned clumsy. I always brought you flowers at the end of an affair, didn't I? Well, you didn't let me in, said you were tired and didn't feel like company, and shut the door in my face. That night I went on the most enormous binge which lasted until I came here. When I got what I thought was your telegram I sobered up for a few hours, then I had a couple on the plane — for Dutch courage. I didn't want to blow it again.' He shrugged his shoulders and opened his hands wide expressively. 'The several whiskies I had here the night I arrived must have been the straw that broke the camel's back. I don't remember going to bed that night, but in the morning I thought I was dying. I knew it was more than a hangover, I've had enough of those lately to remember what they're like.' Quickly he looked at her. 'How did I get to bed that night?'

'Gabrielle and I, with Zoe helping, half-carried you. You were out cold.'

'Zoe saw me?' Roger's voice was sharp.

'Yes, I'm afraid so.

Roger buried his head in his hands. 'I didn't realize I'd sunk so low, to do that in front of Zoe — and Gabrielle, and, of course, you.'

Gently, she put her hand on his shoulder. 'Poor Roger. It must have been a terrible shock to find I'd not sent the telegram. I'm not surprised you hit the bottle again.'

He looked at her incredulously. 'You . . . you're not excusing me?'

She smiled, feeling an affection for him as she'd not felt for many years.

'You really have had a rough time. I didn't realize . . . '

'It was after I left you that I knew how much I really loved you and what I was throwing away. Nothing has been the same since.'

He reached for her hand, which she rested passively between both of his.

'Harriet, can't we begin again? I'll change, I really will. I mean it as I've never meant anything before.' His voice was pleading, tears glistening in his hazel eyes.

Harriet was silent. She looked at their hands, loosely clasped. Deep in her heart was the growing conviction that Carlos would not come back. How could he ever know the truth — there was no way she could contact him in the foreseeable future and she'd be going home in a few weeks' time. No, that episode was over. She took a shuddering deep breath, as a wave of faintness came over her. Roger tightened his grasp on her hand as he saw the pain and sadness vividly expressed on her face. The momentary faintness passed, and Harriet's thoughts raced on to her future, her lonely future without Carlos. She fought down the sudden panic, then raised her eyes to Roger's concerned, waiting face.

'I'm sorry,' she said gently, 'I'm truly sorry, Roger. It wouldn't work'

'But . . . ' his voice was desperate as he seemed to struggle for the words to convince her.

'You see, Roger, *I've* changed.' Her voice was steady, her clasp on his hand firm. 'I'm not the Harriet you married, I'm not even the Harriet I became in the last years of our marriage. I've changed since I've been here in Spain.'

'You mean because of . . . Mendoza. You're still in love with that Spaniard.' Some of Roger's former petulance crept into his voice, quickly stifled.

'Yes, I am. But I know that will come to nothing now.' Harriet kept her voice steady, gentle. She saw the effort Roger was making to control himself and she didn't want to hurt him more than was absolutely necessary. She knew, however, that things must be brought into the open, once and for all. She couldn't let Roger hold out any more hope.

Resolutely she continued: 'I love Carlos Mendoza as I've never loved anyone before. I didn't believe such a love existed or that two people could be so — one. I don't think he'll forgive me for what he believes I did to him,' she quickly controlled the tremor in her voice, 'but having experienced that love, I cannot settle for less. I'd rather spend the rest of my life alone . . .'

She extricated her hand from his, her eyes on his stricken face.

There was a long silence.

Then Harriet broke the tension that was beginning to show for the first time during their long talk.

'What will you do, Roger?'

He raised his head. He'd been staring moodily at the floor.

'Who . . me? I don't know.' He straightened his shoulders and gave a hollow laugh. 'Find myself a rich widow, I suppose.'

'Roger!' Harriet found herself half-believing him.

'No, well, perhaps not. To tell you the truth, I don't need to marry money . . . if I marry again.'

'You will, Roger,' she said quickly, adopting a deliberately light tone. 'You need a woman to look after you. One more patient and less independent than me.'

He smiled wryly then continued: 'The fact is, I've got quite a bit of money put by. It's funny, isn't it? My last deal was a success — the one in Paris.' Harriet's expression showed the surprise she felt. 'I made my pile and then got out with what amounts to a considerable sum, enough to keep us in comfort for the rest of our lives, the children, too. That was one of the arguments I was saving to try to persuade you, Harriet . . . but I realise now that money doesn't come into it at all, does it?'

She shook her head slowly.

He stared at the pool, the tiny waves rippling on its surface. 'I've taken up golf, you know. Yes, me, who never touched a ball of any kind — except at school under pressure. I've got quite good at the game.' He smiled at Harriet's bemused expression. 'You see, people like me can change, the same as you. I was going to suggest we buy a house in the country, you could give up your job — only if you wanted to, of course,' hastily, 'we could potter about, play golf, travel a bit when Zoe goes to University.' Roger paused. 'That doesn't appeal to you, does it? No, I see that now. Not with me, anyway.'

Harriet didn't answer, her mind confusedly looking ahead at Roger in his country tweeds, the life and soul of the local Golf Club, regaling the ladies with wildly exaggerated stores of his exploits — always successful. He'd marry again, perhaps someone much younger than himself, who'd adore him as he needed to be adored, as she had in the first few years of their marriage.

But this time Roger would make sure that adoration would last.

She felt a faint tinge of regret, for what might have been, then dismissed it quickly, welcoming instead the relief and gladness that came over her, as for a child who has at last grown up.

'No, Roger. Too much water has flowed under the bridge.'

She leaned across and kissed his cheek noticing with a smile the faraway expression in his eyes, the growing excitement that always heralded a new 'deal' for Roger.

'Well, then,' he said, carefully rising to his feet. 'I'd better get myself sorted out.

'I'll be alright in a couple of days,' he added briskly, 'then I'd better go. Mind if I use the phone — long distance? A chap in London's trying to sell me a place in Surrey. Plenty of good golfing there.' He walked towards the house with a trace of his old jauntiness.

Harriet felt breathless for a moment. Was this the same man who, only minutes ago, had pleaded with tears in his eyes for a reconciliation?

'Yes,' she murmured to herself. 'That's Roger. In the depths of despair one minute, up in the clouds the next. Zoe's just the same. They'll always land on their feet.'

Smiling to herself she followed Roger into the villa.

★　★　★

At dinner that evening, Harriet was conscious that Zoe was regarding both Roger and herself with speculation.

Her attitude towards her father had changed almost imperceptibly. She'd obviously been distressed by his drunkenness on the first evening of his arrival, having never seen him other than perfect. She seemed to Harriet to be even more determined to bring her parents together, remarking on more than one occasion how lonely her father seemed, how he needed his family.

As Harriet served the coffee at the

end of the meal Zoe said brightly: 'Carlotta and I called in here after we'd taken the children home this afternoon.'

'I didn't see you,' said Harriet in surprise. 'We were on the terrace.'

'I know,' smugly, 'we saw you. You were holding hands and seemed so engrossed in each other, we decided not to disturb you.'

'We were only talking.' Harriet's voice had a faint edge to it. She looked to Roger for confirmation, but he was grinning mischievously at his daughter.

'Roger! Take that grin off your face, for Heaven's sake! You're encouraging her to imagine all sorts of things.' Roger hurriedly straightened his face as she turned to Zoe. 'Actually, Zoe, we were discussing the future . . . ' She paused, considering how best to tell her about their decision, but before she could continue, Zoe said gaily:

'It's alright, Mother. You don't need to explain. It's just as I told Carlotta. You and Dad are getting together again, aren't you?' She half-rose from her chair, arms out-stretched, but stopped when she saw her mother's face.

'You said what to Carlotta?' Harriet's voice was dangerously quiet.

Zoe looked at her uncertainly. 'Well, I've been telling her for ages that it's only a matter of time before you two . . . er . . . Anyway, she saw for herself this afternoon. You were holding hands, and I — we — saw you kiss Dad. I know I didn't imagine that . . . ?' She looked towards her father.

Roger cleared his throat, looking from his daughter's confident face to that of his wife.

Harriet was ashen: 'You had no right to discuss our private affairs with Carlotta,' she said furiously.

'Carlotta's my friend — she's the only person I can talk to here. There's nothing wrong in discussing things with her.' Zoe muttered sullenly. 'I don't know why you're so upset.'

Harriet had gained control of herself. Quietly, she answered: 'There are reasons why I wish you hadn't said those things to Carlotta, reasons you wouldn't understand . . . '

'If you mean because she's Carlos Mendoza's daughter, then I do understand. But that's all over now, isn't it? He's gone away and according to Carlotta he never forgives what he considers an insult or a betrayal. I know it was all my fault, but there's nothing anyone can do now. In fact, I asked Carlotta if she would explain when she writes to him, but she won't. She daren't interfere or even mention it. You know Spanish parents are very different from English ones. Anyway, Carlotta doesn't want you to marry her father. She said he ought to marry Consuela as she's been with them so long. I'm sorry, Mummy, but I agree with her.' Zoe looked defiantly at Harriet, whose face showed the utter despair she felt on hearing her daughter's words.

'Tell me something, Zoe.' Harriet's voice was tired, drained. 'In view of your feelings on the matter, have you been deliberately 'discussing' with Carlotta the possibility of your father and I having a reconciliation in the hope that she would casually mention this in her letters to her father?'

'No, of course not!' Zoe looked at the two accusing faces turned to her, particularly shocked at the condemnation in Roger's expression. 'I've told you. I tried to get Carlotta to help, but when she wouldn't . . . ' her face reddened. 'Well, to tell you the truth I was a bit put out when Carlotta said she didn't want her father and you to marry. I know I agreed with her, but in a funny sort of way I resented her saying it, as though you weren't good enough for her father. So I've been trying to show her that we — Mummy — didn't need him. I didn't think it would do any more harm and I'm quite sure she wouldn't have mentioned you in her letters from what she said . . . ' Her voice trailed off and she looked piteously at her parents. 'You *are* getting together again, aren't you?'

Harriet and Roger exchanged glances. Surprisingly, Roger answered first. His voice was stern:

'Whatever your reasons, Zoe, I think it was indiscreet of you to talk of such things to Carlotta. However, as you've said you meant no harm, we'll accept your word.' His voice softened. 'As for your question — the answer is 'No', dear. Your mother and I, far from having a reconciliation this afternoon, were saying our goodbyes.'

'Goodbyes,' echoed the girl. 'But, I saw you . . . ' her voice broke.

'What you saw and what you surmised, Zoe, were two different things. We were having the first serious talk we've had for years. It was something we should have done a long time ago, but there it is.' He shrugged his shoulders slightly. 'Anyway, the outcome of our talk was that we have decided to go our separate ways permanently. I shall be going back to England the day after tomorrow. Your mother and I will always be friends, I hope.' He glanced towards Harriet. She nodded, smiling gently, still amazed at the change in Roger.

He continued: 'I shall see as much of you and Ben as I possibly can. I'm going to buy a house in the country and you can come and stay with me as often as you like.'

Zoe looked at her mother. Harriet found she couldn't meet the hurt and pain in the girl's eyes. After a brief silence Zoe demanded of her father:

'But don't you mind, Dad? I thought you still loved Mummy and wanted her back. It's her fault again, isn't it?'

This time Harriet met her daughter's hard stare with a steady look of her own, but before she could defend herself, Roger cut in sharply, causing the women to stare at him in surprise.

'No, it's not your mother's fault. It never was. It's time you knew the truth.'

'No, Roger,' murmured Harriet, her hand on his arm. 'She's taken enough.'

He gave her a reassuring pat and went on firmly:

'Your mother has had to put up with a great deal of unhappiness during our marriage, Zoe. I made her very miserable. Not many women would have stayed with a marriage like ours, but your mother did — for your sake and Ben's.'

Zoe's face showed incomprehension, gradually turning to shock as Roger, without mincing his words, elaborated. He spared his daughter little — his unsuccessful, sometimes not quite honest business affairs, his financial dependence on Harriet and her constant worry of keeping him out of prison. Finally he mentioned his women, his constant belittling, criticism and taunting of Harriet, although he didn't go into too much detail of this last, to Harriet's relief. What he did say, was enough.

When he'd finished, Zoe's face was pale. 'Oh, Mummy' she said and burst into tears.

'Leave her a while,' Roger said as Harriet turned as if to comfort the girl.

'She needs time to absorb it all. I hope I've done the right thing, Harriet, but it had to be said. You've carried the blame for too long. I've been a selfish beast,' He sighed. 'She'll never feel the same about me . . . Perhaps it's just as well. He never existed — the father she thought I was.'

12

The next day Harriet made Roger stay in bed, knowing he needed the rest if he was really set on going back to England. She and Zoe had been late retiring the previous night. Zoe had been desperate for Harriet to fill in the gaps of her father's bald statements and Harriet felt she owed it to Roger to be completely honest this time. She excused his behaviour when she felt it was necessary, blamed herself for her own shortcomings but kept to the facts as Roger had done.

She told Zoe of Roger's future plans and stressed to the girl how much courage it had taken for him to tell her the truth, particularly in view of the fact that he loved Zoe more than anything in the world.

Zoe digested all this, saying little, but Harriet could see a new strength in her daughter's face, a maturity that had not been evident before.

As they were at last going to bed, Gabrielle came in looking happier and more relaxed than she had since Ben left. She apologized for missing dinner saying she'd unexpectedly met some friends from London who were holidaying in Malaga. They'd insisted on taking her out to dinner and she'd been unable to telephone until it was too late.

Harriet smiled and reassured her, glad to see her looking so much better. In fact, she'd felt it opportune that Gabrielle had been absent in view of the traumatic turn of events as she would, no doubt, have felt extremely embarrassed to witness the highly-charged emotional scenes that had occurred. And, because of her uncertain status with regard to Ben, she'd probably also have felt intrusive in such a personal family situation.

'What a coincidence meeting friends in Malaga?' she said as the three women slowly went upstairs. 'Are you meeting them again?'

'No, unfortunately they're going home tomorrow, but it was lovely to see them and talk about old times.' Gabrielle's voice was wistful and Harriet knew she was thinking of Ben.

They said goodnight, each one immersed in her own private reflections.

★   ★   ★

'I'm going to see Carlotta, Mum,' Zoe announced getting up from the breakfast table the following day. She dropped a light kiss on her mother's forehead. Harriet nodded absently, feeling a lump in her throat. It was a long time since she'd had any sign of affection from her daughter.

'Will you be in for lunch?' she asked.

'Yes, but I'm not sure what time. Carlotta's going to Paris in a couple of days' time with some friends. I said I'd help with her packing. She's very excited but doesn't know what clothes to take.'

Later in the morning as Harriet and Gabrielle were drinking coffee by the pool, the unfamiliar sound of a motor cycle suddenly shattered the peace of the quiet cul-de-sac. The noise stopped outside the Maxwell villa and seconds later they heard the shrill ring of the doorbell. Wonderingly, Harriet threw a beach wrap over her swimming costume and hurried through the house to open the door.

A young man, whose face was vaguely familiar, wearing denim jeans and tee-shirt and holding a black crash helmet under his arm, smiled shyly at her: 'Buenas dias. Senora Maxwell?'

Harriet nodded, her wayward heart thumping. Could this be a messenger from Carlos? Almost immediately she discovered her mistake, the disappointment leaving her weak and shaken.

'I don't expect you remember me,' the boy continued in strongly accented but good English, 'I was sitting beside you in the aeroplane from England. Your daughter Zoe gave me this address and said I could call here if I was in the area. Is she in?' He was regarding Harriet's white face in some concern. 'Are you alright, Senora Maxwell?'

Harriet hastily pulled herself together: 'I'm sorry, I thought you were . . . Of course I remember you.' She forced a smile to her pallid lips. 'I'm afraid Zoe's not here at the moment, but I'm expecting her back soon. Won't you come in and wait?'

She stood aside to allow the tall young man to enter the hallway. 'I'm afraid I don't know your name. I'm sure Zoe told me, but I have a terrible memory . . . '

'Juan Domingo Hernandez.' The boy introduced himself with a small bow.

Harriet smiled in a friendly way, having regained her own composure and indicated that he should follow her, leading him through the villa towards the poolside where she introduced him to Gabrielle, who gravely shook his hand, a slight twitch of the lips betraying her amusement at the young man's eyes on her bikini-clad body.

'Sit down, Juan,' Harriet said. 'Would you like a chair, or would you rather sit on the floor? Zoe and her brother usually do.'

He chose the floor, placing his crash helmet beside him. There was a small, rather awkward silence, filled in quickly by Gabrielle:

'Would you like some coffee?'

'Yes, please,' he said gratefully.

'Are you staying in Segena?' asked Harriet.

'I'm staying with friends, a few kilometres away,' answered Juan. 'I hope you don't mind my calling here. Zoe said it would be alright.' He smiled his thanks as Gabrielle handed him a cup of coffee.

'Of course I don't mind. Zoe will be delighted to see you.' Harriet sincerely hoped so, but secretly wondered what her daughter's reaction would be to this rather gauche young man. He was extremely good-looking, but since meeting Carlos, Zoe's preference seemed to be for the more mature type of Spaniard.

Harriet regarded him over the rim of her coffee-cup, liking his steady gaze and polite manner, which almost concealed his extreme shyness. She thought it must have taken some effort for him to call on Zoe after so short an acquaintance and felt she should prepare him for any possible coolness in Zoe's manner.

'As a matter of fact, Juan, Zoe isn't very happy at the moment. We've had a little family upset and her Spanish friend Carlotta is going away on holiday soon. Are you staying here long?'

The boy appeared embarrassed. 'Perhaps for a few days, perhaps longer. My . . . er . . . friends don't mind how long I stay with them.' He looked at his hands, which were cradling his empty cup.

For a moment Harriet wondered if

his friends really did exist, or whether he'd come to Segena solely to see Zoe again. Quickly she changed the subject, asking if he'd been on holiday in England when they met him returning to his home in Spain.

She and Gabrielle were interested to discover that he was attending the London School of Economics, which accounted for his good command of English. He was home for the vacation and had been working in his father's business, but had managed to get two weeks off. Apparently his father wasn't too keen on the idea of dispensing with his unpaid assistant and Harriet again wondered if the attraction of Zoe had given him more courage than he would normally show against a strict Spanish father.

Juan was soon chatting quite happily, relaxed by the two women's casual manner towards him. When Zoe returned a little later she was incredulous at the sight of the visitor. She'd obviously forgotten his name, but

Harriet smoothly interrupted the awkward pause by saying: 'Juan was in the neighbourhood and dropped in to see you, Zoe. We've been having a very interesting chat while we were waiting for you to come home.' She turned to the now speechless, moonstruck boy: 'I'm afraid Gabrielle and I must leave you in order to prepare the lunch. You and Zoe must have a lot to talk about. Would you like to stay for lunch? We're only having a light salad, but there's plenty.'

Not waiting for an answer, and avoiding her daughter's despairing glance she took Gabrielle's arm firmly and ushered her into the villa.

Once in the kitchen the two women collapsed into chairs, giggling uncontrollably at the scene they'd left on the terrace.

'Did you see Zoe's face?' spluttered Gabrielle, 'That poor boy . . . ' She stopped laughing suddenly, sympathy for the Spanish boy's predicament entering her voice.

'Oh, dear,' sighed Harriet, wiping the tears of hilarity from her face. 'I know we shouldn't laugh, in fact I don't know why we found it so funny. Reaction from the heavy time we've had lately, I suppose. Anyway,' she added thoughtfully, resting her elbows on the kitchen table, 'I think Zoe's going to get a surprise. There's more to that lad than meets the eye.'

'She'll make mincemeat out of him, he's so obviously got a crush on her,' replied Gabrielle. 'Don't forget she's into the mature, sophisticated type of man now.'

'Juan will be good for her ego, it's at a very low ebb at the moment. She's been hurt by Carlos's supposed rejection.' ('haven't we all',) thought Harriet dismally, as she answered Gabrielle. 'A bit of adoration would do her no harm.'

'But the boy?' Gabrielle wasn't Zoe's mother. 'I hope he doesn't get hurt. You know Zoe doesn't always consider other people's feelings, especially when she's feeling sorry for herself. And since

Roger's revelations yesterday she must be feeling doubly let down by men.' Harriet had related a watered-down account of yesterday's events to Gabrielle, feeling that some explanation had to be given for the subdued behaviour of Zoe and the non-appearance of Roger at breakfast that morning.

'Oh, I think you under-estimate the boy. Beneath that shy manner is someone who knows where he's going. Remember he told us he went to study in England against his father's wishes. He wanted to get managerial qualifications and learn modern techniques before he joins the family business. He's also determined to learn the business from the bottom when he does start. No, I think that once he's got over his shyness with Zoe he won't stand any nonsense from her. Remember too — he's Spanish. Spanish men are accustomed to being the boss. I think it could be interesting — if he's not put off already by Zoe's off-hand manner.'

'I hope you're right.' Gabrielle sounded doubtful.

'Anyway,' said Harriet briskly, getting to her feet, 'It's not up to us. It's entirely their affair, nothing we do or say will make any difference to either of them. Come on, let's get the lunch.'

Lunch began awkwardly, Roger having decided to get up and join them, to Zoe's embarrassment. However, under Harriet's skilful questioning and Gabrielle's purposeful interest, Juan began to throw off his inhibitions and a rare wit and sense of humour emerged. He related family incidents and experiences he'd had in London, especially when he first went there — an inexperienced youth with little English — that reduced them all to helpless mirth and Zoe soon shed her air of bored sophistication towards Juan and coolness with her father, joining in with amusing incidents she'd experienced due to her difficulties with Juan's language.

When, at the end of the meal, Roger

excused himself saying he had preparations to make for his departure the next day, Zoe offered to wash the dishes with Juan's help, with a sly glance in the Spanish boy's direction. Harriet and Gabrielle quickly removed themselves to the terrace.

'Well,' said Harriet, 'what do you think of the boy, now? Do you agree with my opinion of him?'

'Mm . . . perhaps. I think he's a poppet.' Gabrielle laughed. 'Did you see his face when Zoe volunteered him to help wash the dishes?'

'Yes. I think Continental men consider such things beneath them. He recovered well, though, didn't he?'

'You really like him, Harriet, don't you?'

'Yes, I do. I think he's got great potential. I hope Zoe doesn't discard him before she really gets to know him. She's had so many boy friends in London, but no lasting ones. I've always been glad of that, she's still young, but I do think she needs a stable relationship now. Don't get me wrong, I mean just a good friend, someone she can trust, talk to, laugh with and this boy seems to fit the bill. More so even than Carlotta — there was always the barrier of Carlos in that relationship.'

Just then the two youngsters came onto the terrace, Zoe carrying a beach towel in her hand.

'Juan's going to take me for a ride on his motor-bike. We'll probably go to a beach.'

They left, waving gaily, the roar of the noisy machine again momentarily disturbing the peace.

Harriet sighed: 'Oh, to be young and carefree,' she murmured.

Gabrielle regarded her seriously. 'Perhaps that's what you need, Harriet.'

'What? To be young and carefree? Oh, no, I wouldn't be young again really. It's a silly saying, isn't it. The young aren't really carefree. They take everything very seriously and feel very deeply, but perhaps they can be diverted more easily than older people.'

'That's true I suppose for most young people. But I don't mean that. I mean — perhaps you need another man.' The words were spoken carefully, tentatively.

Harriet sat up quickly. 'That's just what I don't need.' She shivered in the heat of the afternoon. 'I've had two serious relationships in my life, and both have ended extremely painfully. I'll never get myself involved that way again.' Her words sounded like a vow and in the following heavy silence, she turned over on to her stomach and buried her head in her arms. Her voice was muffled as she went on: 'What I need is to get back to work!'

Gabrielle was silent.

After a few minutes, Harriet lifted her face: 'What about you, Gabrielle? Have you heard from Ben?'

Gabrielle shook her head.

'What are you going to do? Have you thought about the future?'

'Not really. Strangely enough, I'm not really worried. I still love Ben and I think he loves me. I feel as though I'm waiting. I don't know how long I shall have to wait for him to sort himself out, but when he does, I'll be there. It sounds terrible, doesn't it? I must be the doormat type.' She laughed briefly. 'If I don't hear by the end of the week, I shall have to go home. I need to get some more work, I can't live on air while I'm waiting. It will mean starting from scratch. going round agencies, trying to establish my new image.' She stretched sensuously, demonstrating her lovely figure, more curvacious than when she'd arrived in Spain a few weeks ago, but still slim and lissome. Her elfin face, under the short, sleek cap of auburn hair, was tanned and glowing. Harriet thought how lovely she'd become in such a short time and felt that if Ben were to see her now he'd be sure to fall in love with her all over again.

'I admire your courage and faith. I wish I had some of either, but I can't summon up any at the moment. That's why I need something to do to keep me from going to pieces.' Harriet smiled at the girl. 'I shall miss you when you go, Gabrielle. I sometimes feel you're more my daughter than Zoe. Other times, more my sister, in spite of the difference in our ages.'

Gabrielle smiled back. 'I'm glad you feel that way, Harriet. I wish you were my mother, but then — I couldn't love Ben like a brother.'

Conversation ceased as both women dozed in the sun content in each other's company, little knowing that the diversion Harriet so badly needed was not far away.

13

'Whoever can that be at this hour?' Harriet tumbled out of bed at the shrill sound of the doorbell ringing repeatedly. She glanced at the clock on her bedside table. Seven o'clock!

Hastily putting on her dressing gown she ran towards the stairs, nearly bumping into Zoe and Gabrielle, who were sleepily emerging from their bedroom, alarm written on their faces.

Roger had returned to England the previous day and Gabrielle had decided to go home on Saturday. Harriet and Zoe would spend the next two weeks on their own, as they'd begun the holiday, though closer together than when they'd arrived.

Quickly Harriet opened the door to find Carlotta standing outside in great distress, the three young Mendoza children huddled sleepily behind her.

'Carlotta! What on earth's the matter?' demanded Harriet, opening the door wider to usher them inside.

'It's Consuela. She was taken ill in the night and the doctor has said she must go to hospital. She has appendicitis. The ambulance is arriving in a few minutes.' Carlotta was distraught. 'I must go with her, but the children . . . ' Her voice trailed off as she looked pleadingly at Harriet. 'Would you mind looking after them until I get back?'

'Of course I will, Carlotta. Poor Consuela. Is she in great pain?'

'Yes, I'm afraid she waited too long. She didn't want to worry me. She thought the pain would go away. We have to go to Malaga. I will return on the autobus. I'm afraid I don't know how long I shall be.' The girl spoke in quick disconnected sentences, her English plainly taxed in her distress.

Turning to the children she spoke to them firmly in Spanish. They nodded in reply looking disconsolately at the floor, clearly bemused by the sudden turn of events.

With a last wave Carlotta disappeared and Harriet took Maria's hand and telling the boys to follow, led them into the warm, sunlit kitchen, where they were joined by Zoe and Gabrielle who'd been hovering at the top of the stairs and had heard Carlotta's explanation.

The children had obviously been dressed hurriedly and by the way they were avidly looking at the breakfast table which Harriet had prepared the night before, had had little or nothing to eat.

Pointing to chairs round the table, Harriet hastily cut chunks of bread, placing them in front of the children and pushing the large pot of strawberry jam towards them. They needed no further prompting and were soon eating ravenously.

'Milk?' asked Gabrielle and they nodded, cheeks bulging. They were just finishing when Juan arrived to take Zoe out.

By the time Harriet had packed a liberal supply of sandwiches, salad and fruit for the young couple, thinking of Juan's pocket, Zoe had appeared in jeans and teeshirt and they made their departure.

The Mendoza children soon found themselves back in the routine formed on their previous visits and Harriet was surprised how quickly her close relationship with the children was re-established.

By the time Gabrielle returned from shopping Harriet was stretched lengthways on her stomach beside the pool with the children drawing pictures on large sheets of paper with crayons she'd bought in the market the previous week.

'There's another sheet of paper for you, Gabrielle. Come and join us,' laughed Harriet.

'No thanks, the competition's too good for me,' replied Gabrielle as she admired the children's lively pictures and laughed at Harriet's excellent cartoon-like drawings of the children. 'I think I'll go and get us something to eat.'

The children were asleep in the shade on sunbeds when their sister returned from the hospital. Harriet gently pushed the weary girl into a chair and, on learning that she'd had nothing to eat all day, quickly prepared a light snack which Carlotta ate gratefully and ravenously.

Afterwards she told them the news of Consuela, which was worrying and serious. As soon as they'd arrived at the hospital, peritonitis was diagnosed and Consuela was rushed to the operating theatre. Fortunately they'd been in time, but Consuela was still rather poorly. Carlotta had stayed at the hospital during the morning and at Consuela's bedside afterwards. She was still recovering from the anaesthetic, sleeping deeply. The doctors had advised Carlotta to return home and to telephone during the evening when Consuela would be awake.

'Anyway,' concluded Carlotta, 'they are confident that she'll be alright, which is a good thing. I can't help thinking, though, what would have happened if we'd been any later. If I hadn't woken early and heard Consuela groaning. She would not have called me and, one hour later . . . ' Carlotta buried her head in her hands and sobbed, exhaustion making the worry and ordeal of waiting at the hospital even worse. 'I'm sorry, Mrs. Maxwell,' she said at last, blowing her nose and wiping her wet cheeks. Harriet had felt it best to let the girl weep, holding her in her arms as she would have held Zoe.

'There's no need to apologize, dear. You've had a bad day and done well not to break down before now. You should have had someone else with you, perhaps either Gabrielle or I should have come with you . . . '

'Oh, no, Mrs. Maxwell,' broke in Carlotta, 'I'm so grateful that you were looking after the children. That helped so much not having to worry about them, too.'

Seeing the girl looking more relaxed and cheerful after the release of tears, Harriet decided to bring up a matter which had been on her mind since the girl had left to go to the hospital. 'Carlotta, weren't you supposed to be going on holiday tomorrow?'

'Yes,' replied the girl sadly. 'My school friend and her parents were taking me with them to Paris for two weeks. But, of course, I cannot go now. I must stay and look after the children. I intended to telephone them from the hospital but I was so worried about Consuela that I forgot.'

'I was wondering,' mused Harriet, her casual tone disguising the excitement she felt. 'I was wondering whether you need to cancel your holiday after all?'

'But . . . the children?' The Spanish girl looked at her in puzzlement.

'I could look after the children for

you. It seems such a pity for you to miss your holiday. Zoe told me how much you were looking forward to going to Paris.' Harriet held her breath while she waited for the girl's reply.

'Oh, Mrs. Maxwell, that's very good of you, but I couldn't possibly . . . and there's Consuela, she won't have anyone to visit her . . . Oh, no, I couldn't . . . ' Carlotta's voice trailed off, a tiny note of hesitation and hope creeping in.

'I could take the children to the hospital to visit Consuela when she's feeling a little better,' said Harriet. 'That's no problem. And the children — they'll be fine with me, you know they like it here and they are used to me so it's not as if I'm a stranger. Why don't you think about it? Go on home, have a bath and relax. What time had you arranged to leave tomorrow?'

'They're coming to collect me tomorrow at about five o'clock in the evening.' Carlotta sounded bemused. She regarded Harriet's eager face again.

'But you couldn't visit Consuela. You don't even like her.'

Harriet was taken aback at this, as she thought her own attitude towards the Spanish woman had always been carefully courteous.

She said: 'We haven't seen enough of each other to be very friendly, but I feel very sorry for her at the moment and seeing the children will be more important to Consuela than any contact we might have. And talking of Consuela, I think she would like you to take your holiday. I can't help feeling that was the reason she didn't call you earlier when she was in such pain.'

'Yes, I think you are right. In fact when we were in the ambulance she said she was worried about my holiday and asked couldn't I find someone to look after the children.' Carlotta's voice held a trace of amusement, despite her concern. 'I don't think she considered you, though.'

'Probably not,' Harriet grinned in return. She paused, then continued, her heart in her mouth. 'Is there someone else — a friend of the family, who would look after them?'

Carlotta was definite. 'No, most of our friends are away on holiday themselves. The ones who are left, well, I don't think the children would be very happy staying with them for two weeks. They are old and not used to small children . . . '

Harriet breathed a sigh of relief. 'Well, then. I'm the only possible person.' She gently pressurised the girl. 'I'm sure Consuela will make a better recovery not feeling guilty about you. Would you like me to come to the hospital with you tomorrow and talk to her myself?'

Carlotta was half-convinced and beginning to look hopeful. 'I'll telephone the hospital in about an hour and ask if I can see Consuela tonight. If she agrees to the idea perhaps you would come to see her tomorrow?'

Harriet had to be content with that, although privately she felt that even if the Spanish woman had no objections she would still be feeling and looking very ill and Carlotta would have fresh qualms about leaving her.

The girl left a little later taking the three children and promising to telephone Harriet as soon as she'd contacted the hospital.

'You must be mad!' exclaimed Gabrielle when they'd gone.

'Why? Having the children or promising to visit Consuela?' replied Harriet humorously.

'Both. You're supposed to be on holiday. Now look at you. You might as well be back at work. That would be much more relaxing.'

'But it's what I need, Gabrielle. The answer to my prayer. I can't be idle now. I'll go crazy!'

'Idle, yes. But to take on the whole family . . . There's Zoe, too, although she could help you I suppose . . . Perhaps I should stay a bit longer?'

'No, that's not necessary, although it's sweet of you to offer. You must go back to England, you said so yourself. Honestly, Gabrielle, I really would enjoy having the children — they'll stop me thinking of Carlos all the time. That's what's driving me mad.' Harriet's voice was desperate and Gabrielle touched her hand gently.

'I can see you're determined and I won't try to change your mind any more. But promise me, if you find it all too much, or you need a shoulder to weep on, let me know and I'll fly back immediately.'

Harriet was affected by the girl's concern, but all she could say was: 'Ben's such a fool!'

'I agree, but now I know where he gets his stubbornness from — and it's not his father!'

★　★　★

Later that evening Carlotta telephoned to say that Consuela was still very sleepy after the operation and the hospital didn't advise visiting until the following day. She added: 'The doctor told me that Consuela is quite well and there is no cause for concern. She needs a lot of rest now and will have to stay in hospital for at least two weeks. Oh, Mrs. Maxwell, I still don't know what to do. I wish I could talk to my father and ask his advice.'

Above the sudden beating of her heart, Harriet's voice was casual: 'Can't you get in touch with him?'

'No, he only left a forwarding address at his office. Consuela sends our letters there. In case of an emergency his secretary has a list of telephone numbers to use. I telephoned the secretary's home just now but her mother said she has gone away for the weekend.'

'But surely, in a real emergency . . . ?'

'Senora Lopez, the mother of father's secretary gave me the telephone number of the hotel where her daughter is staying at the weekend, but it's a long way away and she won't be arriving until midnight. I don't want to cause too much bother or he'll come home and that's not necessary. Consuela didn't want to call him either when I suggested it in the ambulance. His business is very important. Why else would he have gone so suddenly?'

Harriet could have told the distraught girl why her father's departure had been unexpected. She was tempted to advise her to bring Carlos home, but knew the girl's sense of duty was too strong. She would rather miss her own holiday than disturb her father's important business.

Harriet sighed inwardly, but answered cheerfully enough: 'Don't worry, Carlotta. There's nothing you can do for Consuela, she's in good hands and the children will be alright with me, I promise you. You go and enjoy your holiday. Have you spoken to your friend's parents yet?'

'No, I decided to telephone them after I'd spoken to you.' Carlotta was infected by Harriet's optimism. 'I will tell Consuela tomorrow when I go to visit her.'

'Shall I come with you?'

'No, the hospital said only one visitor would be allowed tomorrow. Thank you for offering. Anyway I think it would be best if I went alone. I'm still not sure how she'll accept the idea.'

'Well, Gabrielle will drive you to the hospital, I'm sure.' Harriet looked questioningly at Gabrielle who was listening with interest to Harriet's side of the conversation. She nodded vigorously in agreement.

'That would be very kind — it is a long way and very tiring on the autobus.'

'That's arranged then. Bring the children across in the morning as soon as you're ready.'

14

The next ten days raced by.

Gabrielle had telephoned twice in the first few days, but for over a week now there had been no news from her. In spite of her preoccupation with the children, Harriet was beginning to feel some concern. Ben had not been in contact since he'd left, although this was not unusual. He'd always been an erratic correspondent mainly on account of his job, taking him away at a moment's notice to test a new car in remote parts of the country. Harriet had received an unexpected letter from Roger a few days after he left, a sad, rather poignant note apologizing for the trouble he'd been whilst in Spain but reaffirming his hope that they would be friends. He gave her the address of the house he was buying, asking if she would write occasionally. He also wrote that he hoped Zoe would write to him and hoped she had forgiven him. Harriet showed the letter to Zoe, who made no comment except to ask if she could keep the letter so she could write down the address.

Emily had also written several letters since Harriet had been in Spain, all full of news and local gossip from the village where Emily now lived with her sister, Beatrice. The last two letters seemed to express concern over Harriet's welfare, which puzzled Harriet as she'd always tried to keep her own letters cheerful and light-hearted, saying nothing of the traumas and unhappiness she'd suffered. There would be enough time to discuss those when she returned to England.

Sitting alone one evening in the comfortable living-room, the children asleep early after a particularly exhausting day on the beach and Zoe and Juan at a disco, Harriet was composing a reply to Emily's latest letter. She suddenly realized this would be the last letter she would write to Emily from Spain as she and Zoe would be returning the following week.

Next week! She'd not realized. Time seemed to have no meaning here, especially now. The children . . . how could she bear to leave them? And Carlos? Suddenly she knew that deep in her heart she'd not accepted that she would never see him again. Every time she heard the telephone ring or a step outside the door, a tiny part of her mind leaped, to be quickly stifled.

And why had he gone? She thought of Zoe, happy with her young friend Juan, making plans to see him when he came to England in September. Zoe had no dreams of Carlos now, Harriet was sure. How long had that great love lasted? A week? Maybe a little more. Carlos had been right.

If she'd not hesitated when Zoe first told her she loved Carlos but revealed the true situation immediately, would all this have happened? True, the telegram had already been sent to

Roger the day before, but would Carlos have so readily believed the worst of Harriet? It had been her doubts and hesitations and finally her insistence on waiting until Zoe had got over her infatuation that had made Carlos conclude that Harriet sent for Roger in desperation. Admittedly, she had allowed Carlos to persuade her to tell Zoe that evening, but the damage had already been done.

It was all her own fault, but had she been completely wrong? Sitting still and quiet now, for the first time for several days, Harriet knew she couldn't have, wouldn't have acted differently, even had she known the outcome.

Now it was too late. She had no way of contacting Carlos, not knowing his office number, to pass a message to him. Consuela knew. But she could never ask Consuela unless it was a dire emergency, such as the illness of one of the children, Heaven forbid!

Harriet had taken them to visit the hospital several times, but after rather stilted greetings and Harriet's one-sided attempts at conversation, both women sat back and allowed the children to take over.

Consuela's health was improving slowly and she seemed to be enjoying the rest in her luxurious private room at the hospital. She had the care of the best doctors and the attention of several nurses. Harriet remembered Carlos telling her that Consuela had some money of her own left by her parents and here at the large hospital, it showed. She seemed to express no great desire to be back home, except at times her lips would compress when the children talked of 'Senora Harriet' or little Maria cuddled up to the English-woman when she tired during the long visits.

Once Consuela remarked she thought the boys were getting out of hand after a rather noisy argument they'd had over sharing some sweets, a comment Harriet thought a little unfair as she knew that the children were, in fact, far better behaved in the short time they'd been with her than they'd been before. But she knew Consuela was still feeling weak after her operation, so made no comment herself. However, she warned them before the next visit of Consuela's still-delicate state of health and ever afterwards their behaviour was impeccable.

No, she couldn't ask Consuela.

Anyway, Carlos had been so angry, so hurt, he would probably ignore any attempts she made towards a reconciliation. It had to come from him.

★　★　★

'Look, there's a photograph of Carlos Mendoza in the newspaper!'

Harriet's eyes flew open and she strained her ears to listen to the young couple who were stretched out on the terrace a few yards from the lounger. The children were asleep in the shade, tired from the morning's activities and the heat of the afternoon sun.

'What does it say, Juan?' Zoe was looking teasingly over Juan's shoulder, as he read the Spanish newspaper that he'd brought with him that morning. He flicked the paper away in mock-irritation and she tried to snatch it back from him, resulting in a bout of laughing horseplay which landed them both with a splash in the pool.

'Be quiet, you two, you'll wake the children.' Harriet's voice was tense in spite of the lightness she tried to assume. She's not mentioned Carlos since the heart-to-heart talk she'd had with Zoe a couple of days before Roger's departure. Zoe had then tearfully apologized for the trouble she'd caused by sending the telegram to Roger, and the hard and angry words she'd spoken to Harriet. She seemed to assume that Harriet had forgotten Carlos as quickly as she had herself. There had been no reason to tell her otherwise and the unhappiness Harriet still felt was deeply hidden. The sound of his name a few minutes ago was enough to make Harriet's pulses race and she realised how vulnerable she still was.

Zoe and Juan climbed out of the pool, quiet now but still thumping each other playfully.

'What was that you said about Carlos Mendoza, Zoe?' Harriet asked casually.

Zoe picked up the discarded newspaper and showed her mother a photograph of Carlos with a very beautiful dark-haired woman, both dressed in evening clothes and obviously enjoying each other's company, by the intimate way they were holding hands and smiling into each other's eyes. A stab of jealously went through Harriet, making her feel suddenly sick. She closed her eyes.

Zoe had turned to Juan who was drying his hair briskly with the towel he'd been lying on.

'Come and translate for us, Juan,' she ordered, handing him the newspaper and indicating the short paragraph written in Spanish beneath the picture.

'It says 'Is this to be Dona Isabella's third husband?' ' The boy's voice was casual, bored. A wave of faintness swept over Harriet. Through the mist she could hear Juan's voice as he continued to translate:

''The beautiful Dona Isabella Marguerita Constanza' .. um . . . you don't want to hear all the names, 'escorted once again by Senor Carlos Mendoza of the wine-exporting firm of Mendoza and Sons. The handsome couple, frequently seen together recently are causing a great deal of interest in social circles in Madrid. A very good friend of Dona Isabella told the writer an announcement is expected soon. Senor Mendoza lost his wife in tragic circumstances two years ago. Since then he has lived in Southern Spain away from the social scene. Has the fair Dona Isabella been the one to bring him back again?' '

Juan finished reading. Zoe's mouth was open as she gazed at him in amazement. Neither noticed the pallor and distress on Harriet's face as she fought for control of her senses and emotions.

'D'you know them?' Juan was looking at Zoe with interest.

'Him, not her,' Zoe answered briefly. She grinned: 'You've only been throwing his sons into the swimming pool this morning.'

'His sons . . . ' Juan was incredulous. 'Is that who their father is? I never thought . . . Mendoza is quite a common name . . . but Carlos Mendoza of Mendoza's the wine exporters. Madre de dios! My father knows him. His family is one of the oldest in Seville. He's very rich. I wonder why he lives here? He used to own a fantastic villa in Madrid, then they moved to Granada just before his wife was killed in that car accident. That was headlines in many papers. Lots of rumours and hints, but I cannot remember the details.'

Zoe was dazed: 'Very rich . . . and well-known, too. Mother, did you hear that?' She turned to Harriet. 'Why, what's the matter, Mummy?' at last noticing her mother's extreme distress. 'Are you alright? Oh, God! . . . ' She dropped on her knees beside Harriet's lounger and put her arms round the distraught woman: 'Oh, Mummy, I'm sorry. I didn't realize . . . I thought it was all over between you . . . ' Her daughter's sympathetic words and loving manner were too much for Harriet. Tears streamed down her face as she sobbed on Zoe's shoulder.

Juan stood watching in bewilderment. Then muttering 'I'll go and get a drink,' he disappeared into the kitchen, leaving them both in tears, Zoe's more from sympathy for her mother's grief than for any deep feelings of her own, although perhaps a trace of what she had once thought possible coloured her feelings.

After a few minutes Harriet succeeded in controlling herself and forced a shaky smile to her lips.

'I'm sorry, darling. It was such a

shock, hearing his name in such circumstances. I've been feeling a bit low, lately, with the thought of leaving the children and I hardly slept at all last night. I didn't mean to upset you.'

At that moment Juan emerged from the kitchen, a tray of cold drinks in his hands.

'Thanks, Juan,' Harriet smiled faintly at the boy. 'That's very thoughtful of you. What must you think of us crying all over your newspaper.'

'That's alright, Mrs. Maxwell. We Spanish are quite used to such things. It was just a bit surprising to see you . . . you know, the cold English . . . ' the boy's words trailed off as he shrugged in embarrassment.

'Oh, yes. We're not supposed to be emotional or to show our feelings, are we? Well, now you know differently. Our stiff upper lip fails us sometimes.' Harriet reached for her drink and sipped it gratefully and Zoe, still regarding her mother anxiously, followed suit.

Juan was obviously still rather puzzled at their strange behaviour, but was too polite to ask questions. He showed relief when Zoe finished her drink quickly and stood up. 'Let's go and swim.'

After that incident all hope in Harriet died.

15

Towards the end of the holiday, and a few days before the return of Carlotta from Paris, Zoe announced they should have a party. Juan was enthusiastic as he always was with Zoe's ideas, but Harriet put forward numerous objections. She was too tired, too busy, they didn't know enough people, parties were expensive. Zoe brushed these aside with determination and at last, when Harriet was assured that Zoe and Juan would organize everything, she resignedly offered the use of her cheque-book. At first she tried to summon a little interest in the project, half-listening to the youngsters arguing amicably, but very soon left them to themselves, devoting her daylight hours to the children.

This was a poignant time for Harriet, knowing she'd probably never see the children again after she returned to London. Contact between the two families would be impossible, except perhaps between Zoe and Carlotta. She discussed the return of Carlotta and Consuela with the children, building excitement and anticipation. She talked of her own and Zoe's departure to London casually, getting them used to the idea so it would not be too much of a shock for them, especially Maria who had become particularly attached to Harriet. They all seemed to accept the situation but one day, Maria, sitting beside Harriet and struggling with wool and knitting needles said: 'You're not really going to leave us, are you, Senora Harriet?'

'But I must, Maria. I've explained it to you. I have to go to England to my work and to see Ben and Gabrielle.'

'You won't go away. I know you won't.' The piping voice was confident. Harriet was unable to reply, her heart full. How do you convince a child of something it refuses to know? she thought despairingly.

The subject wasn't brought up again by any of the children, and Harriet, feeling cowardly, took their lead and left it for the time being.

Zoe had been frantically busy baking for the party, talking on the telephone for hours, Harriet had no idea with whom, and a couple of times disappearing, with Juan for several hours on mysterious missions. Harriet was really too disinterested to question their activities.

On the morning of the party and Carlotta's return, Zoe said after breakfast: 'We need to reorganize the bedrooms, Mother. Do you mind moving to the small room? It will only be for a couple of nights?'

Harriet regarded her daughter in astonishment: 'What on earth for?'

'The guests, Mum,' she spoke patiently. 'Your bedroom is the largest and we can fit a couple of people in there.'

'What people? And why for two nights?'

'They're coming a long way and they might as well stay over the weekend.'

'Surely your friends can use sleeping bags, we've got several in the cupboard. And I don't see the necessity for giving up my room.' Harriet felt a flash of annoyance. She'd agreed to the party, but having to move to another bedroom for the sake of Zoe's friends was really too much!

'I'm giving up my room, too. Oh, please, Mum.'

Harriet looked at her daughter's pleading face. It hadn't been too much of a holiday for the poor child, what with Ben and Gabrielle breaking up, her father coming and going, Carlos . . . , the children's take-over of the villa, Harriet's apathy and unhappiness . . . Juan had been the only bright part of Zoe's holiday.

Harriet sighed: 'Alright, Zoe. Only for two nights, though. We're going home next week and I've got to have a good sort-out of the villa before we go.' She paused as a thought struck her.

'How many people are coming, by the way?'

Zoe grinned airily: 'I'm not quite sure of the actual number, but there will be quite a few. Don't worry, we'll fit them all in.'

'Well, as long as I can go to bed reasonably early and not be disturbed by the noise, I can probably put up with the inconvenience.' Harriet smiled at her daughter: 'This is going to be quite a party, isn't it?'

'Yes, Mum. Quite a party. By the way, what are you going to wear?'

'Me? Oh, I don't know. I hadn't thought about it. It's your party, no-one will notice what I wear. Probably my black dress, it's the only one I've got.' Harriet tried to inject a little enthusiasm in her voice.

'What about the blue one you wore to the Mendoza's. It looked super.'

'Not that one!' sharply. 'I've torn it, and . . . it's dirty . . . I spilt some wine on it.' Harriet's voice trailed away as her daughter regarded her quizzically.

'No, not that one, Zoe.'

Zoe bit her lip, obviously vexed at her tactlessness. 'Sorry, Mum.' There was a small silence, then Zoe continued. 'Look, why don't you go to Malaga and buy a new one? I'll look after the children. It won't take all that long to get there. You could be back by lunch-time. Or stay and have lunch there. Really, Mum, it will do you good. You haven't been anywhere for ages.' As Harriet looked doubtful, her daughter pursued. 'Anyway, I don't like you in that black dress. It makes you look . . .'

'Old?' broke in Harriet, humorously.

'No, not old — cold, formal. Not you. You need something gayer. Please, Mum, just for me.'

'Oh, alright. I could do with a change. Maybe I will buy something.' Harriet got up to wash the breakfast dishes, but Zoe took them from her hands.

'Go now, Mother, before you change your mind.'

As Harriet walked through the

235

beautiful old town, looking in the attractive shop windows, she felt a slight revival of interest. She'd always enjoyed shopping, especially for clothes. Trying on several of the dresses displayed in the boutiques aimed at the tourists, her mind wandered. She'd been leading a very narrow existence this holiday, especially the last few weeks. Her world had revolved around her own family and that of the Mendoza's. She really had to pull herself together. Zoe was right to nag her. She smiled at the thought. A reversal of roles had taken place with Zoe taking on the responsibility for the running of the house, while she, Harriet, had buried herself in the children's activities. It was pure escapism on her part, she knew, and strangely so did Zoe, who actively encouraged her, shooing her out of the house when her conscience brought her inside to cook a meal or wash the dishes.

She felt a prickling behind the eyes as she thought of the change in Zoe, from a petulant, spoilt adolescent, to the mature, perceptive young woman she was becoming. Although fortunately, thanks mainly to Juan, Harriet felt, the young tomboy still came bubbling through when the occasion demanded. So much had happened in a few short weeks!

Harriet's own natural bouyancy began to surface and, resolutely handing back the dresses she'd taken from the rails of the boutique, she crossed the wide street and entered the portals of the most exclusive gown shop she could find. There, displayed in the centre of the salon, was the dress. Deep rose chiffon, with shoe-string straps. Deceptively simple. Deceptively expensive, too, I'll bet, and not at all suitable for Zoe's party, thought Harriet, looking in vain for a price-tag.

'Senora looks beautiful!' exclaimed the assistant, calling her colleagues to the fitting room to admire the English lady. Harriet stood self-consciously smiling whilst the Spanish girls chattered excitedly round her, adjusting a fold here, a flowing drape there.

She spent a further hour and many more pesetas on matching shoes, then returned home, exhausted but triumphant.

'No, you're not going to see it. It's a surprise.' She laughingly pushed away Zoe's eager hands and, after giving the equally excited children the sweets she'd remembered to buy, went upstairs.

'Don't forget you're in the small bedroom,' Zoe called after her.

'What, already?'

'I'm still doing the other rooms, and they're in a mess.'

Containing her curiosity, Harriet avoided her own bedroom and put her purchases on the single bed that had been Ben's, then Roger's and was now hers for the next two nights.

She looked round. Zoe had transferred Harriet's toiletries to the dressing table, which was polished to a mirror shine. A small bowl of flowers fresh from the garden rested in the centre of the low, round table and books and magazines with a small basket of fruit were displayed on the shelf under the window. Everything, in fact, to make Harriet feel at home. She smiled to herself at her daughter's thoughtfulness and, slipping off her shoes with a sigh of relief, sank on to the bed. Ten minutes, she promised herself, ten minutes before she retrieved the strings of the household from Zoe's capable hands. It was time she came back to the world of the living.

Carlotta arrived at one o'clock. She looked happy and excited, and hugged the exuberant children who were pulling at the parcels they knew she'd brought for them. Pressed into joining them for lunch, Carlotta told them about her holiday and the wonders of Paris whilst the children unwrapped, tested toys, and shrieked delightedly in the background.

When, at last, Carlotta had finished

relating her holiday experiences, 'for the time being,' as she laughingly threatened her captivated audience, the subject of Zoe's party was mentioned. Carlotta was a little quiet at first, then she said: 'Are you sure you want me to come, Zoe? I won't know any of your friends, and you'll want to talk to them. You haven't seen them for a long time.'

Zoe regarded her friend sternly: 'Nonsense. Of course you must come. Anyway, it's partly a welcome home party for you.' She pulled a protesting Carlotta into the house. Juan, who'd been helping the children try out their toys, looked after them in amusement, declaring to no-one in particular. 'Women!'

Harriet said worriedly: 'Poor Carlotta. She's so shy. I can understand her reluctance to come to the party. There'll be no-one she knows — unless, of course, Zoe has invited some of her friends, too. I think she met several when she used to go to the beach with

Carlotta.' Harriet looked at Juan for confirmation.

Juan was evasive. 'It's alright, Mrs. Maxwell. Zoe will persuade Carlotta. Honestly, she'll be really glad to come when Zoe's talked to her . . . ' He looked at his feet and coughed, his face reddening.

'What is going on, Juan?' Harriet asked in puzzlement. 'I hope Zoe's not going to do anything foolish. Have you met these friends of hers?'

'Some of them.' Juan had recovered himself and grinned at Harriet. 'They're alright. Don't worry.'

But Harriet was beginning to worry, remembering the mysterious new friends that Zoe had wanted to join in Greece for the holiday. Surely not them! Her worries didn't completely disappear when Zoe and Carlotta emerged from the house, arms entwined. Carlotta looked slightly bewildered and glanced strangely at Harriet before saying she thought it was time she took the children home. She thanked Harriet sincerely for taking care of the children whilst she was on holiday and a further few minutes was taken up with finding them as they'd, predictably, hidden themselves away as soon as they knew they were going home.

When at last they were rounded up and kisses exchanged, Harriet said: 'We'll see you tonight, then, Carlotta? And I'll see you children tomorrow when Carlotta brings you to see me.'

'We're coming to the party, too,' said little Fernando as he turned to go, but his words were lost in the hubbub of farewells and Harriet followed Zoe and Juan into the house.

16

Car doors slamming outside her bedroom window woke Harriet.

Sliding out of bed she peered through the half-open shutters at the near darkness outside. Two taxis were in the process of turning, ready to depart having obviously unloaded some of the guests for the party. Zoe's guests must be pretty well-off, she thought incuriously, there were plenty of buses into the village, which was only a short walk to the villa complex. Shrugging her shoulders, she reached for her toilet bag and going to the bedroom door cautiously opened it slightly, peering out.

Juan was seated on the floor at the top of the stairs, reading. There was no sign of anyone else and no sound could be heard from downstairs. Opening the door wider, Harriet made for the bathroom.

Juan looked up quickly, closing his book.

'What on earth are you doing there, Juan?' Harriet demanded pausing in her tracks to regard the boy, who appeared ill-at-ease. 'Where's Zoe? Did I hear some of her guests arriving?'

Twisting the book between his hands, Juan answered: 'I'm the look-out. Zoe's downstairs. She told me to tell you not to come downstairs yet. She said to get yourself ready.' He smiled at Harriet nervously, obviously embarrassed at having to deliver Zoe's instructions.

'That young lady goes too far sometimes,' replied Harriet rather crossly. She felt like a puppet, everyone seemed to be pulling her strings, even young Juan, not that he looked too happy about it.

'I'll have words with her when I get downstairs,' she continued, turning again towards the bathroom. 'Alright, I'll play her little games. But I warn you, I shan't stay long at this little party you two have cooked up between you.

244

I've got a good book and I'll retire to my room as soon as I get the chance.'

When she emerged after a long leisurely bath, Juan was still sitting at his look-out point. He peeped at her from under his long, black lashes, looking as young as Fernando and Pepe. Harriet laughed, her good humour restored at the sight of him.

'You're making sure of me, I see,' she grinned. 'It's all right. You can go now. I promise I won't peep.'

Juan didn't move, continuing to read his book. Still smiling, Harriet entered her bedroom.

As she carefully but lightly made up her face in front of the tiny mirror, she remembered the last time she'd dressed up for the evening. The dinner at Carlos's villa. She closed her eyes against the sudden pain. So much had happened since then . . . Opening her eyes quickly she told herself: 'This is Zoe's party. Don't be a wet blanket, for goodness sake.'

There was a slight tap at the door

and Juan's voice called: 'Are you ready, Mrs. Maxwell?'

Bracing herself, she answered: 'I'm just coming,' and opened the door.

Juan was transformed, hurriedly it seemed by the dishevelled state of his hair, into smart grey trousers and a crisp white shirt. Grinning, he offered his arm to Harriet. 'You look wonderful, Mrs. Maxwell,' he breathed in admiration.

Indeed, Harriet felt herself to be looking especially good. She had no idea why, when she felt so unenthusiastic about the forthcoming evening. The rose colour of the chiffon dress suited her dark colouring to perfection and gave her rather pale cheeks a reflected glow. Even the faint shadows that had reappeared under her eyes in the last few weeks were not so noticeable in the soft electric light.

She'd been tempted to have her hair set whilst in Malaga, but felt there wasn't really time. As her hair had grown longer since she'd arrived in

Spain, she was now able to draw the dark curls back from her face, exposing the exquisite bone structure and making her shadowed eyes appear even larger and more luminous.

She gave Juan a mock curtsey and, taking his arm, they walked slowly down the stairs.

Juan knocked on the living room door, behind which Harriet could hear subdued giggles and scuffles. 'Oh, God,' she thought, 'they're not at it already!'

Assuming a rather disapproving expression on her beautiful face, she entered the room behind Juan.

'Ta-ra-ra!' Zoe's voice rang out and Harriet stared in amazement, immediately dropping the pose of heavy mother she'd mischievously adopted at the last minute. There were flowers everywhere, spilling over vases, in glasses, bottles, every container that could be found had obviously been used.

But Harriet saw only the faces in

front of her — Zoe, smiling happily, Ben and Gabrielle, arms around each other, obviously rapturously reunited and, no, it couldn't be — Emily, sitting solidly on the settee, her sister Beatrice beside her.

'Ben, Gabrielle — I'm so glad to see you both ..' They hugged her, laughing at her bemused expression. 'Emily, Beatrice, how lovely! So that's why I had to leave my bedroom,' she smiled at Zoe as she went forward to kiss her old friends with affection. Standing in the middle of the room, sipping the wine that Juan had handed to her, she said to her daughter: 'You monkey. I thought it would be all *your* friends ... ' Her voice was husky as she surveyed her son and his fiancée and her own dearest friends. Tears threatened to spill down her cheeks.

'Now Mother,' warned Ben, 'you'll spoil your make-up.'

Everyone began talking at once, and Emily whispered to Harriet; 'We'll talk properly later, my dear. It's so lovely to see you. You look very attractive in that dress.' Harriet squeezed her hand affectionately.

The doorbell rang. 'That'll be Carlotta and the children,' Zoe sounded relieved as she rushed to the door.

Harriet kissed the excited children, now dressed in their Sunday clothes and looking like angels. She then greeted Carlotta, who unexpectedly kissed her on both cheeks, saying shyly: 'Hello, Senora Harriet. You don't mind me calling you that, do you?'

'Of course not, Carlotta,' smiled Harriet, folding the girl in her arms.

'Well,' she said in a choked voice, looking round the smiling assembled party, 'it's so lovely having all my friends and family together . . . '

'Wait a minute,' called Zoe, who, Harriet thought with affection, was becoming extremely bossy. 'We're expecting another guest. Where's Consuela?' she asked Carlotta.

'Consuela!' Harriet's heart sank. Brightly she smiled at the Spanish girl.

'I didn't realize Consuela was home from the hospital.'

'Yes, she came home this morning. She . . . er . . . said she would come for a little while tonight. She's just coming, Zoe,' Carlotta turned to the other girl. 'A button came loose just as she was leaving. She told us to come on ahead.'

The doorbell shrilled again. 'That must be her now,' Carlotta's voice faded away and there was a sudden hush in the room. No-one moved.

'I'll go,' said Harriet quickly, breaking the silence, but Ben forestalled her. 'No, Mother, you stay here.'

He stood at the door for a second before opening it, looking round at the assembled party. 'Ready?' They all nodded. Harriet, still standing in the middle of the room, felt a sudden shiver pass over her body.

Ben opened the door. Consuela stood there, rather paler than usual, but wearing an unaccustomed smile on her face. Harriet's eyes flew beyond her and the room began to spin.

She felt someone's hand on her arm, and Gabrielle's voice whispered in her ear. 'Steady, Harriet.' The room righted itself and there he was, magnificent as ever in his white evening jacket. Harriet saw only his dark eyes, filled with anxiety and love.

'Carlos?' she whispered.

He held out his hands and at once the room seemed empty but for the two of them. 'Oh, Carlos,' she breathed again as she went towards him and his strong arms engulfed her. How long they stood there holding each other, saying nothing, Harriet couldn't tell, didn't care, but it felt like a lifetime.

Some time later, their other world intruded in the shape of two champagne-filled glasses thrust at them by a smiling Ben.

Carlos drew Harriet on to the settee next to Emily and sat close beside her.

'How did . . . ? Who . . . ?' Harriet looked from one to another of her assembled guests, happiness making her more beautiful than she'd ever been.

Carlos could not tear his eyes from her face and held her hand tightly as if afraid she'd disappear.

'It was Zoe.' 'No, it was Ben.' 'No, Emily.' Everybody began talking at once, until Harriet held up her hand, laughing in confusion. Zoe said quickly, 'Quiet everybody. I think we'd better put Mum out of her misery and explain.'

'Yes, please,' Harriet begged. Little Maria, after regarding her father and Harriet silently for a long time, had climbed on to the settee and managed to wedge herself between them, holding their hands and resting her head on the touching bodies. The boys were sitting on the floor between their father's and Harriet's feet. She thought her heart would burst as she looked at Carlos and his children and felt herself so tightly bound to them. A soft voice behind her whispered: 'Welcome to our family, Senora Harriet,' and Carlotta kissed her, putting her arms around them both from where she was standing behind the settee.

'Come along now, you Mendozas, you can't have her yet, we haven't finished,' Zoe grinned at the little group.

Carlos's hand tightened on Harriet's as the story began to unfold.

'It was Emily, really, who began it,' said Zoe quietly.

'Emily?' Harriet looked in surprise at her friend, who nodded and smiled, carrying on from Zoe's opening remark.

'Yes,' she explained, 'I'd had these strange letters from you, Harriet. Not many, I must say, and that was peculiar in itself, you're usually such a regular correspondent. The letters were not in your usual chatty style, they were patchy as if you were searching for something to write about, or trying not to say too much. Almost from the start you mentioned Senor Mendoza.'

'But I didn't,' broke in Harriet, 'I was very careful not to mention . . . ' she stopped in confusion.

'I know you, Harriet Maxwell. You

253

said very little about him, but still managed to bring his name about five times in a two-page letter.' Everyone laughed.

'I could read behind the lines and I knew something had happened. You were happy, excited, then the tone of the letters changed and suddenly you didn't mention him at all. I was worried when there was a long time gap with no letter, so I rang Ben to find out what was the matter. Ben?'

Ben cleared his throat. 'Well, selfish beast that I am. I knew nothing. I was so wrapped up in my own problems.' He looked tenderly at Gabrielle who was sitting on the floor beside him, holding his hand.

'But,' Ben went on, 'Emily insisted there was something wrong. I then hazily remembered how quiet you'd been at the dinner at Carlos' villa and how excited you were the next day just as I was leaving for England. You said you had something to tell me but decided it would wait until later. I was pretty upset at the time and didn't press you. Anyway, I thought I'd better get in touch with Gabrielle, as some friends of ours who had met her in Spain told me she had arrived back in England a few days before.'

'You wouldn't have phoned me if it hadn't been for that,' teased Gabrielle, a rueful smile on her face.

'Perhaps not just then, I was still a bit uncertain about how I felt. We arranged to meet,' Ben continued, turning back to his wider audience at the same time putting his arm round Gabrielle, 'and as soon as I saw her I realized what a fool I'd been, a proud, stubborn fool.'

'He wasn't the only one,' whispered Carlos in Harriet's ear. She leaned even closer to him, gently putting her fingers to his lips.

Ben was still talking. 'After Gabrielle and I . . . talked a bit,' he grinned sheepishly, 'I managed to get her to tell me about Mum and Carlos and the whole story came out. We went to see Emily and she was furious. Especially with Zoe.' Ben looked across at his sister sternly.

Zoe was quiet for a moment, the happy smile now gone from her face. She took a deep breath and looked at her mother: 'I'm not very happy about my part in the beginning of this, as you know Mummy . . . anyway, Emily rang the villa last week when you were out with the children. When she knew I was alone she laid into me, as only Emily can.'

Harriet smiled sympathetically at her daughter. Emily chuckled beside her, but no-one spoke.

'Well,' continued Zoe, 'Emily asked me what I was going to do about it. I told her there was nothing anyone could do, it was all over. 'Nonsense,' Emily boomed down the phone. Zoe's voice was an almost perfect reproduction of that former headmistress's brusque tone. Everyone laughed, including Emily and her quiet sister.

Zoe's voice had gained in confidence. ''What about the Spanish lady?' Emily then asked me. 'She must know how to get in touch with Senor Mendoza. As you know it's no good arguing with your friend Miss Preston when she's determined, Mother, so Juan and I went to see Consuela in hospital.'

They all looked at Consuela. She was sitting in an upright chair, her face calm and beautiful, feet close together and hands clasped loosely in her lap.

'Do you want me to go on, Consuela?' asked Zoe.

'No, thank you. I can manage.' Consuela's English, though not as perfect as Carlos and his daughter, was adequate. 'Zoe came to see me, as she said, with her young friend,' she indicated Juan with a slight incline of her head. 'I was very surprised to see them. I thought at first something had happened to one of the children. But no, Zoe asked me if there was any way she could contact Senor Mendoza — Carlos. I had a telephone number for an emergency and an office address, but I wasn't sure if I could give it to her. Carlos had given strict instructions. I could only give the telephone number to one person who asked for it.' Consuela paused. 'Senora Maxwell.'

Harriet gasped. Her eyes flew to Carlos. He nodded.

Consuela was continuing with her part of the story. 'But Senora Maxwell didn't ask either for his telephone number or his address. Nor did she mention Carlos, except once and that was to ask me not to tell him she was looking after the children. She said she felt it would only worry him unnecessarily. I was inclined to agree with her. In fact, he didn't know I was in hospital. Carlotta and I had already decided there was no need to mention the fact, unless, of course, it became absolutely necessary.

'However, I naturally thought Senora — Mrs. Maxwell didn't wish to contact Carlos, and it certainly wasn't up to me to offer her the information. Carlos's instructions were quite precise — only if she asked me herself. He said nothing about her family. I asked Zoe what she wanted to discuss with him and I would contact him on her behalf.'

Zoe broke in: 'And I didn't know if I should tell Consuela. After all, it was your personal affair, Mummy.'

'I am surprised,' commented Harriet dryly, 'everyone else seemed to know.'

'Well, they were family, at least Emily's nearly family, but Consuela . . . I'm sorry,' Zoe smiled winningly at Consuela, who surprisingly smiled back.

'I quite understand,' the Spanish woman said. 'To continue. Zoe returned the next day saying she'd contacted Ben and Miss Preston and they had decided she must tell me the whole story.

She paused and looked steadily at Harriet. 'I was very surprised, to be quite frank with you. I didn't have a very good opinion of Mrs. Maxwell. I felt she was rather . . . er . . . frivolous, I think the English word is, for a . . . not young English lady.'

There was a shocked silence, broken by Carlos saying with amusement:

'Well, Harriet, you did have on that scanty bikini when Consuela first met you and your dresses are a bit revealing . . . ' He lewdly peered down her cleavage. The room erupted as Harriet blushed, trying to cover herself with her hands.

'Spanish ladies, especially after a certain age, are not in the habit of exposing their bodies as English ladies seem to.' Consuela's voice was firm. Everyone's face straightened hurriedly as Consuela carried on. 'I thought Mrs. Maxwell was trying to seduce Carlos — as so many ladies do, even Spanish ladies.' Her lips were pursed in disapproval.

Carlos tried to look modest, succeeding only in grinning fatuously. Harriet gave him a wicked look.

Consuela continued, ignoring the by-play between the lovers: 'When I heard Zoe's story, I revised my opinion slightly and I felt that Carlos should know the truth about the telegram. Fortunately he was in Madrid, so I had little difficulty in contacting him.'

'I know all about Madrid,' muttered Harriet to Carlos. He raised his eyebrows questioningly. 'Later,' she whispered ominously.

'Quiet, you two,' remonstrated Zoe, her ebullience completely restored. 'Thank you, Consuela. I think you should say your piece now, Carlos.'

'What here, in front of all these people?' Carlos looked horrified.

'No, not that, silly,' grinned Zoe, 'your part of the story.'

'Oh, yes. Well, where shall I start?' He shifted his body and put his arm round Harriet. 'I won't go into all the details. Enough to say I was very upset that day, thinking you had sent for your husband to rescue you from my clutches.' They looked at each other wordlessly for a moment. 'Well, I immersed myself in my work, travelling all through Europe meeting with my customers and associates. All the time I was hoping you would get in touch with me if you still loved me, but no word came. Then Carlotta wrote that your husband, ex-husband, was still staying at the villa and that you seemed very close. She wrote that Zoe had told her that you were going to be reconciled.' His voice deepened. 'It was hell!' There was a long silence. Harriet felt the tears brimming in her eyes. His arm tightened on her shoulder. 'Then I had the phone call from Consuela when I was in Madrid. I couldn't understand at first, the reports seemed conflicting. If Zoe had sent the telegram why was Maxwell still at the villa, weeks afterwards, and why did Carlotta write that she saw you holding hands and kissing him? So I told Consuela to get Zoe to telephone me. There was no way I could come home just then, I was in the middle of a very important business conference involving our company in a great deal of money. And, to be honest, Harriet, I was still a little suspicious.'

Harriet had noticed that Carlotta,

now sitting on the floor with Zoe, had gone a little pale at the telling of Carlos's part of the story, especially when he mentioned the letters she'd written to him. Knowing the former feelings of Carlos's daughter on the liaison between her father and Harriet, fortunately now completely revised, Harriet realized Carlotta now felt guilty at her manipulation of the truth by concealing Roger's illness from Carlos and by elaborating on the supposed reconciliation.

Gently shaking her head as the girl attempted to interrupt her father, Harriet managed to convey a warning to say nothing for the time being. There was plenty of time for explanations and self-recriminations later. She knew that neither she nor Carlos would ever, by word or suggestion, blame either daughter for her part in the affair.

Carlos was continuing: 'Among other things, Zoe told me how upset you were when you saw my photograph in the newspaper, Harriet. The woman who was with me, Dona Isabella, is a very old friend of mine, we grew up together. Reports of our marriage were grossly exaggerated. I know that lady far too well to hold any romantic notions regarding her. I remember it amused us both considerably when we read the newspaper report. I had no idea you would see it, as it was in Spanish.'

He looked troubled as he made the simple explanation, remorseful at having given pain to his beloved Harriet. She smiled back at him, the memory of that pain erased from her mind by the feeling of deep content and trust in their love.

'One thing I can't understand, though,' she said, her brow wrinkling in puzzlement, 'if you only spoke to Zoe yesterday, what about all this?' She indicated the flower-filled room, the assembled party of family and friends.

Zoe piped up once again: 'Masterly organization on my part,' she declared modestly. 'Or to be perfectly honest

— pure coincidence. When we were talking on the phone last week, I suggested to Ben and Gabrielle that it would cheer you up if they flew over to tell you themselves that they'd got together again. Then when Emily heard, she said she'd like to come over with Beatrice so we decided to have a party. We didn't really know then what would happen about Carlos, but as you can see everything fell into place.

'I persuaded him, much against his will, not to come here straight away.' Zoe grinned affectionately at Carlos. 'He nearly ruined it all by sending all those flowers. Fortunately they arrived — a whole van-load — when you were in Malaga this morning.'

'I wondered where they came from,' exclaimed Harriet, admiring again the masses of roses, carnations, mimosa — in fact every flower that was in bloom somewhere in Spain had been included and seemed to fill every available space in the room.

Carlos laughed: 'As Zoe forbade me

to come to you until tonight, and I could see how determined that young lady can be . . . ' he pretended to cower, 'I had to do something to fill in the time. Seriously, though, it did give me the opportunity to bring my meetings to a rapid conclusion and cancel everything for the next few weeks.' He looked meaningfully at Harriet, who smiled happily back. 'I've got far different plans now — there's a wedding and a long, long honeymoon to organize.'

'Before you both rush off to find a priest, I think we ought to eat. I've spent hours in the kitchen preparing this marvellous feast and I won't have it wasted for anyone.' Zoe led them all into the dining-room and, dramatically whipping off a covering cloth, disclosed a table laden with goodies, suitable for both Spanish and English tastes. The children were soon tucking in to their favourite dishes and the grown-ups, hungry and thirsty after the long explanations laughingly followed suit.

After they'd eaten, Emily suddenly stood up, her glass in her hand.

'I'd like to propose a toast to the happy couple — Carlos and Harriet. We wish you every happiness.' Everyone echoed the wish, raising their glasses.

Harriet looked at them all, tears very close to the surface.

'Thank you everyone, for all you've done to bring Carlos and me together again. And thank you especially, Consuela. You needn't have helped, but you did and I'm very grateful. Without you . . . ' Harriet's hand tightened on Carlos'. 'Well, all I can say now is . . . this has truly been a family affair . . . I know we'll always be one large, happy family now.'

She glanced at Carlos and the expression on his face and sudden darkening of his eyes as he looked at her made her body tremble, her cheeks glow with sudden heat.

Carefully getting up from the settee with the now sleeping Maria in her arms, she moved across the room to

Consuela and handed the child to her.

'I hope you will stay with us, Consuela. The children need you, and so do we.' Was that a tear in Consuela's eye as she quickly looked down at the sleeping child? Harriet couldn't tell. She wondered fleetingly if the Spanish woman was in love with Carlos. She'd probably never know the truth about Consuela's feelings, but the children loved her and hopefully she would help Harriet bring them up in the Spanish way as was their birthright.

Consuela smiled at Harriet over the child's head — a wintry smile, but a beginning. Perhaps, after all, they did understand each other, as only women could, without the necessity for long speeches.

She turned to the others. There was so much to talk about to Ben and Gabrielle, to Emily and her shy sister, to Zoe for arranging this wonderful party . . .

But not now. She kissed the sleepy boys and Carlotta, then turned to

Carlos, taking his outstretched hand.

Pulling her closely against his side, he smiled at the other occupants of the room. 'I second everything that Harriet has just said. And now that you've all finished arranging our lives, for which I will be eternally grateful, would you mind if we both slip away. We have a great deal to discuss. Ben, I wonder if you would mind seeing Consuela and the children home. She must be feeling very tired. It's been a long day. Carlotta, would you put the children to bed?'

'Can Juan and I come and help you?' asked Zoe, quickly. Carlotta was delighted and preparations for the leave-taking began.

Turning to Harriet and speaking softly under the covering distraction of the sudden activity in the room, Carlos nodded towards the door. 'My car's outside, shall we go for a drive?' The look in his eyes made Harriet's heart pound as he continued: 'Where shall we go, querida?'

Smiling into his eyes she answered: 'There's a little beach not far from here . . . '

THE END

Other titles in the
Linford Romance Library:

LOVE WILL FIND A WAY

Susan Darke

Sara is an hotel receptionist until her friend Caroline, a resident, helps her into a new job — as a secretary at her son Redvers' flower-farming business in the Scillies. When Redvers eventually whispered, 'I love you, Sara', she should have been elated. But an inner voice mocked her — telling her it would be more truthful had he said, 'I love you, *Miranda*' . . . Was he merely using her as a shield against a love that had once betrayed him?

FAR LIES THE SHORE

Marian Hipwell

Calanara was an island with a secret. What caused the rift between Tansy's mother and her grandfather? And why was the hostile Mark Harmon opposed to her plans for Whitton Lodge Nurseries? Probing past events helped Tansy to find solutions to the problems of the present, only to discover that there was no place for her on the island. Yet something about Calanara called to her and the longer she stayed, the harder it became to leave . . .

LOVE'S FUGITIVE

Rachel Ford

Exploring the French Pyrenees was meant to be a complete break for Victoria, as well as inspiration for possible future work, after her recent traumatic experiences . . . It didn't work out that way — drugged and robbed, she awoke to find herself at the mercy of Gilles Laroque! As lord of the manor he wielded considerable power: Victoria found herself trapped and made to 'pay her dues'. To an independent woman, the situation was unbearable . . .